"Not all marriages fail."

"They say fifty percent fail, but I think that number is closer to eighty."

Jaslene put her forefinger on his chest. "Maybe you should try to get past your divorce."

Cal was about to slide his arm around her and give her a kiss she wouldn't forget. "I am past it."

"No, you aren't. You think every woman is as untrustworthy as your ex."

"Not every woman." *Only the ones who cheated.* He left that unspoken.

Rising up onto her toes, she said in a husky tone, "I didn't cheat."

He wasn't sure if she deliberately encouraged him or if her attraction led her, but he didn't question. He just slid his arm around her waist, pulled her against him and kissed her.

He felt her stiffen and heard her sharp indrawn breath. But if she felt the same fire as him, she'd go with him on this expedition. Sure enough, she relaxed against him and moved her lips with his.

* * *

If you're on Twitter, tell us what you think of Harlequin Romantic Suspense! #harlequinromsuspense

Dear Reader,

Falling for a man jaded by love can be scary even in real life, but in fiction it makes for great conflict. Nobody wants to get hurt and a wall of protection around a man's heart can be a challenge to break through. Jaslene breaks through Cal's with finesse in *Cold Case Manhunt.* She's the determined friend of a missing woman who is thrown together with the detective helping her solve the case.

I enjoyed writing this book so much because the winning over of hearts was fueled by an intense search for a killer. I hope you share the wonder.

Jennie

COLD CASE MANHUNT

Jennifer Morey

HARLEQUIN® ROMANTIC SUSPENSE

Recycling programs
for this product may
not exist in your area.

ISBN-13: 978-1-335-66215-6

Cold Case Manhunt

Copyright © 2019 by Jennifer Morey

Printed in U.S.A.

www.Harlequin.com

Two-time RITA® Award nominee and Golden Quill award winner **Jennifer Morey** writes single-title contemporary romance and page-turning romantic suspense. She has a geology degree and has managed export programs in compliance with the International Traffic in Arms Regulations (ITAR) for the aerospace industry. She lives at the foot of the Rocky Mountains in Denver, Colorado, and loves to hear from readers through her website, jennifermorey.com, or Facebook.

Books by Jennifer Morey

Harlequin Romantic Suspense

Cold Case Detectives
A Wanted Man
Justice Hunter
Cold Case Recruit
Taming Deputy Harlow
Runaway Heiress
Hometown Detective
Cold Case Manhunt

The Coltons of Roaring Springs
Colton's Convenient Bride

The Coltons of Red Ridge
Colton's Fugitive Family

Visit Jennifer's Author Profile page at Harlequin.com, or jennifermorey.com, for more titles.

For Mom and Dad,
who are together in the afterlife now.

Chapter 1

The soothing pendant lighting and upscale atmosphere of Pinocchio's in Chesterville, West Virginia, didn't cast its usual charm without Payton Everett. Sitting on a leather bistro chair with two of her other friends, Jaslene Chabot would never again joke about their *Sex and the City* bond. They were one woman short.

Tatum Garvey stirred her speared olives in her martini glass. "I think it's time to let her go," Catherine Starr said.

"I can't let her go." Jaslene missed Payton terribly and she couldn't live with the torture of not knowing what had happened to her friend, a reporter for a local newspaper with ambitions, fiery red hair and green eyes. She loved reporting on community issues, ranging from Good Samaritans' deeds to personal injustices.

"I can't, either," Tatum said. A tall, stunning blonde, she'd started her own interior design business and had been featured in a popular home magazine. She dressed to match the part without trying. She had an eye for style. "But why haven't the cops found her yet?"

Payton had been missing for seven months.

"You two do realize that Payton is dead," Catherine said. "Right?"

The wife of a successful insurance broker, she had two kids and was trying for a third. She wasn't as tall as Tatum, but she had pretty dark hair and sparkling gray eyes. She had a way of stating what she thought without censor. While Jaslene took offense, she couldn't dispute the possibility. She just didn't want to face that yet.

"You don't know that for certain," Jaslene said.

"The detective told you the case had gone cold," Catherine said.

He'd called her to tell her, as if doing so would make her back off. "Yes. I'm going to go see him tomorrow."

"You've gone to see him a lot and it doesn't seem to do any good."

Jaslene eyed Tatum in disgruntlement. No amount of pushing made the case move forward. She couldn't will it to, either, which highly frustrated her. There weren't any real leads. Payton's car had been found at a park. Had she gone for a walk and something happened? She was not the type of person who would run off. Something had to have happened to her, something bad.

"If there is no evidence, no detective alive can make it magically appear," Catherine said.

"So, you both are just going to…give up?" When both her friends didn't respond, she grew incensed. "How do you think Payton would feel about that? Her closest friends throw up their hands and *assume* she's dead and turn their backs and go on with their lives and forget all about her?"

"That isn't fair," Tatum said. "We *need* to go on with our lives. That doesn't mean we'll forget about Payton. She'll always be one of us." She spread her hand palm up in a half circle from Jaslene to Catherine.

"I will *never* give up." Even Payton's family had stopped looking. They waited for news from Jaslene, but they had lost hope.

Catherine reached over and put her hand over Jaslene's. "You were always the closest to her."

Jaslene slid her hand away, not understanding how Catherine and Tatum could give up so easily. She saw her friends from a different perspective. She had always thought they'd stick together. No matter what. Now that Payton was gone, that no longer applied. It was as though she had been the glue that held the four of them together.

"Well." Jaslene took out her wallet and put some cash on the table.

"Jaslene," Tatum protested. "We aren't turning our backs. We have jobs and families. We can't take a leave like you did and you have no one waiting for you at home."

She had taken a leave from her job as an environmental geologist and she was single, but that didn't mean she wouldn't have done the same if she'd been in a relationship.

Jaslene stood. "I suppose there's no point in continuing these get-togethers."

"You're being melodramatic," Catherine said. "Of course we should keep meeting. It's not like we aren't still friends because Payton isn't here anymore."

Jaslene leaned forward, putting her hand on the table. "I'm going to find Payton. Dead or alive." She straightened. "You two don't have to help."

"Jaslene…" Tatum protested.

"Don't go like this," Catherine said.

Jaslene turned and walked away.

Neither Catherine nor Tatum tried to stop her. Maybe she was overreacting. But all she had to do was think of how Payton must have, or possibly still, suffered and she had no question in her mind. She would not, not ever, give up. If Payton was still alive, her friend would not want anyone to stop looking for her. And while she most likely was dead after being missing for so long, Jaslene had to know for certain. She would not quit until she did.

She would make the police keep looking and she would push and push and push until they worked as hard as they could to find her. The police assumed she had been abducted somewhere in the park, but there had been no witnesses. No one had seen her there and no one had seen her arrive there.

"Chief wants to talk to you."

Calum Chelsey looked up to see the Chesterville

chief of police's assistant standing in front of him, with a cup of coffee.

"What for?"

"Didn't say." She turned and walked away. Alice was a prickly sort, tall and skinny with black-rimmed glasses and hair that was always in a tight, black ponytail. He'd heard she was married and had two kids and hoped she was a different person outside of work. Happier.

He stood from his desk and walked to the chief's office, knocking on the open door.

Chief Moran waved him in. "I emailed you a new case."

Cal stopped before Moran's desk. Great. Another case to add to his already full workload. He didn't mind the amount of work; in fact, most of the cases would be easy to close.

"The mayor wants it resolved as quickly as possible. You know Christopher McBride? He owns that coal-to-fuel plant south of town?"

"I know the plant."

"His son was killed two nights ago. Shot after leaving a bar. I'm putting you on the case. Only work this, no others."

"What about the missing person case?" That was the only case that interested him. In truth, he'd been feeling under-challenged in the department.

"I've reassigned it."

That came as a shock to Cal, and a huge disappointment. Had the chief done so because it had gone cold the week after Payton had gone missing, or was it because the request came from the mayor? "Why me?"

"You're the best detective I have. I know I can count on you."

"Why is it so important?"

"The mayor wants it solved ASAP."

Cal didn't like that. He didn't respect anyone who put a person's social standing ahead of crime solving, ahead of victims. "In other words, this Christopher McBride thinks he's more important than Payton Everett and her family?"

The chief pointed at him. "Don't start with me."

"I can work the Everett case, too." Cal turned and would have left.

Chief Moran said, "Only the McBride case."

This was what he hated about working for a police department: orders. That and lack of integrity. He'd voiced his honest opinions more than once and knew he'd brushed close to getting fired. He was never fired because he was one of the departments top detectives.

Cal slowly faced the chief. He could not back down now. "I'm not going to stop investigating the Everett case."

The chief stopped shuffling papers on his desk and met Cal's eyes squarely. "What's that I just heard?"

"Who'd you assign the case to?"

"Walsh."

Walsh didn't have the experience to take on a case like that. "Don't bother. I can handle both the McBride and Everett cases."

"This isn't about what you can and can't handle,

Chelsey." The chief's voice rose with his triggered temper. "This is about what the *mayor* wants. Now go get to work. I've already told McBride you were the best man for the case. He's waiting to talk to you in the conference room."

Cal didn't move. A few days ago, he'd received an offer to join a private firm: Dark Alley Investigations. They had just opened a satellite office in Chesterville and thought that Cal would be a valuable addition. They had contacted him in the past as well, but Cal hadn't seriously considered it until lately. This was the final nudge to push him over the fence.

"Then you'll have my letter of resignation by the end of the day. I'm working the Everett case." Turning once again, he left the office with a wave of relief and the sense that this was the right thing for him.

"Chelsey."

The chief went to his office door. "Chelsey!"

Cal kept going, noticing other workers stop what they were doing to look and see what the commotion was about. He ignored them all. As he reached the conference room, he saw a man in a black suit standing inside. He spotted Cal and walked to the door as though to greet him.

"Detective Chelsey?"

Cal could see the arrogance in McBride's brown eyes. He didn't smile and definitely seemed grief-stricken. Losing his son to murder put the darkness there but hadn't dimmed the aggression.

"Detective Chelsey?" a woman suddenly called.

He recognized the voice and almost closed his eyes

in annoyance. They were coming at him from all directions.

"Chelsey's going to win a popularity contest today," one of the other detectives quipped.

He heard Jaslene Chabot rushing his way. He turned to see her marching toward him, golden-blond hair flapping behind her sexy body.

"I've just been told nothing will be done on Payton's case. It's been moved to another detective?"

He doubted she'd been told nothing would be done. She must have made that assumption. "The case has been reassigned, yes. The new detective will work on it."

"Why not you?"

Cal glanced at Mr. McBride. "I've been assigned to a new case."

"But…it was my understanding that you have the most experience in this department."

"That's why he's working on my son's murder," Mr. McBride said.

Jaslene's pretty blue eyes moved to that man and then back to Cal. "Payton could have been murdered, too. Why is this case more important?"

"It's not."

"He's already said another detective is working your case," Mr. McBride said impatiently, then turned to Cal. "Now, if we can get started. I'd like to go over my expectations."

His expectations?

"Who the hell do you think you are?" Jaslene said. He'd gotten to know her fiery side the very first time they'd met. At first he had been struck by her attractiveness and then they had fallen into a professional relationship, with Jaslene determined to find her missing friend and concerned only about that.

Cal held up his hands. "Hold on a minute. First." He looked at Mr. McBride. "I'm turning in my resignation today." Then he looked at Jaslene. "Second, nobody's case is more important than the other. The only people I care about are the victims." He turned back to Mr. McBride. "I suggest you remember that."

"What?" Mr. McBride put his hands on his hips. "You're what? Quitting? You can't do that."

"If you want my services, you're going to have to go through Dark Alley Investigations." With that he turned and walked away.

He reached his desk and sat, ready to begin typing his resignation. Jaslene appeared at his desk. She looked contrite.

"Why did you quit?"

"I haven't yet." He poised his fingers over the keyboard. "But I'm about to."

She sat on one of the two uncomfortable metal chairs on the other side of his desk. "Why?"

"Because I'm going to solve the Everett case."

"Don't I have to hire you for that?"

"DAI is a nonprofit organization. I can do what I want. The main purpose is to catch killers."

"But I can still hire you."

"Yes."

"I will, but only if you let me help you."

He could see the determination in her eyes and in the

way she held herself, legs crossed, back straight, hands stacked on her leg. Deceptively prim. The thought of working with her every day both gave him a sexual spark and made him wary. Aside from being quite demanding in the search for her friend, she was also standoffish. There were moments when he sensed her attraction to him but she always reined it in before anything progressed into something acknowledgeable—the other side of her fiery spirit. What would he find underneath her ice queen shell?

"You don't have any experience," he said.

"I want to be involved."

"Don't you mean you want to boss me around?" he half teased.

She sighed in exasperation. "I'm not normally like that. Payton is my friend."

She never let him forget that. He thought her tenacity was actually refreshing, almost as appealing as her prettiness.

He wouldn't encourage her, though. "You've made that abundantly clear…on many occasions." He started typing. This would be a short letter.

Alice appeared beside his desk. "The chief wants to see you again."

"I'm sure he does. Tell him I'll be there in five minutes."

When Alice left, Jaslene sat back against the chair, her posture not so rigid anymore. "Look, Detective Chelsey, I know I've been pushy. It's just that…" She sighed and looked away. He thought he saw moisture gather in her eyes before she blinked the emotion into submission. "Last night I met my friends for drinks and they told me I should let Payton go. They don't think Payton will ever be found. They think she's dead. They've been saying for a while now that they think it was her stalker."

"Riley Sawyer?"

She nodded, still visibly upset.

Cal had checked Riley out early on, having read in the police report that he had dated Payton for almost a year. When she ended the relationship, he began following her everywhere and parking outside her house, looking into windows. She had gotten a restraining order against him. Things had escalated, with him breaking into her house and pleading for them to get back together. At the time, Payton had been on the phone with Jaslene, who'd called the police. Riley had been arrested. That was the last time he'd attempted to see Payton.

"He is still a person of interest in my mind," Cal said. "He had a weak alibi and he had motive. But there's no concrete physical evidence tying him to the crime, as you know."

"Too well."

There had been no sign of a struggle, no blood, no prints, nothing broken. Nothing. That had been the frustration with this case all along.

"My friends have given up. I haven't," she said.

"They're probably concerned over how obsessed you are over the case."

"I wouldn't call it obsession."

Cal refrained from comment, but Jaslene watched

him and must have picked up on the general direction of his thoughts.

"I've known Payton since high school. We went to the same college, where we met two other friends and rented a house together. Payton and I did a lot together. We were going to get married on the same day in the same church and have kids the same age. Tatum and Catherine don't understand. They haven't known her as long as I have."

"Well, I understand." He understood about not giving up on the missing. Not giving up on the dead.

Her eyes softened, full of relief and gratitude. Her mouth lifted in the most tender smile, and he was enraptured.

"Have you eaten lunch yet?" he asked.

"No."

"Why don't we go grab something and talk about how we're going to proceed?"

Her smile broadened, snaring him further. "Okay."

"I just need to resign first."

She laughed. "I'll wait for you outside."

Jaslene did not expect Cal to turn out to be such a warmhearted soul. Whenever she met him before, he had always been professional and only focused on the case. Today his demeanor seemed…more personal. Maybe being freed from the police department had done that. She had always thought he was the best detective for Payton's case. He had done more than anyone else in searching for her.

She believed him when he'd said he only cared about

the victims. He also showed compassion for her. She hadn't expected that, or the sudden flash of attraction that had come over her. She'd thought he was a good-looking man from the very beginning, but she had been so intent on finding Payton that it hadn't mattered.

Now Cal had quit his job and was joining a private investigation agency, taking Payton's case with him. He'd become her champion.

He came out of the station with the same hard set to his eyes she'd always found so unreadable. Now he just looked sexy. Six-four with dark hair and blue eyes a shade lighter than hers, he dressed in slacks and a suit and tie. When he'd first introduced himself he'd said, *I'm Detective Calum Chelsey, but call me Cal.*

"There's a good deli just up the street," he said.

"Okay." She walked with him, feeling self-conscious of her appearance. Did she look good enough? Why did she worry about that when she was with him?

"Are you from here?" he asked on the way.

"Yes. My family lives here. You?"

"No. I'm from Texas. I like not being close to my family."

"Black sheep, huh? My family is very close. I'm the second youngest of four very different people who all got varying professional degrees." Talking eased her nerves. Why was she nervous anyway?

At the deli, they ordered and found a table next to the window. Although a clear day, it was chilly and she could feel the cold air radiating inside. Winter had set in early this year. She saw snowflakes and dead leaves blow across the street, whipped up by passing cars.

"What about you?" Cal asked. "You said you were a geologist but what do you do?"

"I'm an environmental geologist. I work with renewable energies at a consulting firm."

"Interesting."

"I've always loved earth science. At the risk of sounding insensitive, in college, I was not very interested in the environment but those were the hot jobs at the time. I care about the environment, but as a science it isn't very fascinating. I need that kind of stimulation. I don't do meditation well. Sometimes I think I should have gotten into seismology or something."

"You would have had to move away from Chesterville. Not much earthquake activity here."

She smiled. Moving away had never occurred to her. She enjoyed being with her family, especially her parents. She couldn't imagine not being able to stop by for tea in the sunroom with her mother. They could talk for hours.

"Why don't you like your family?"

"I like them…well, sort of." He grinned. "My dad loves the NRA and ranching. He's ex-military, so he was always very strict. That I didn't mind so much. Guns have their usefulness but being an NRA fanatic goes too far in my opinion. My younger brother loves guns, like my dad, and capitalism. They are both executives at the same oil company. Corbin followed in Dad's footsteps. They are both very successful. I never wanted to be an executive. I wanted to make more of a difference than a ton of money. My dad and I had a lot of arguments about my career choice."

"What about your mother? Surely you like her."

He chuckled briefly. "Of course. She didn't have to work, but the ranch keeps her busy. She always let Dad make all the big decisions when it came to us. I guess I resented her for that, but not anymore. She was a great mom."

He seemed to like his family more than he let on. He might have a rift with his father and maybe his brother, but what family didn't have their differences?

"Is it just you and your brother?" she asked, wondering why she was so curious. They had never talked like this before.

"I have a little sister. She is the ranch manager. I'm probably closest with her."

"And you're a homicide detective." Jaslene pondered that a moment. "Why?"

"My grandfather was murdered. He was in a convenience store when some robbers arrived. He tried to stop them and one of them shot him. I was very close to him. It changed me. Losing him that way."

"I'm so sorry." She could feel his sorrow. Even after all these years he still missed his grandfather. Jaslene averted her gaze as she thought of her own loss. Her husband had been murdered, too. Before that all-too-familiar pain overtook her, she smothered it as she usually did.

"It made me want to go after every thug who hurt anyone," Cal said. "I still do. Joining DAI will allow me to help more people who have nowhere else to turn. That will give me the most gratification."

She had sensed that in him early on, his determination to catch criminals. He had gone after Payton's missing persons case with an aggression she had not seen in other officers. She had never doubted him when he said the case had gone cold. She had despaired numerous times but had never had any reason to fault him. He had left no stone unturned.

As they finished and left the restaurant, Jaslene marveled how much things had changed in less than a day. This morning she hadn't thought much of Cal Chelsey. Now she saw him in a completely different way. Maybe it was his understanding over the way she felt about losing Payton. Maybe it was his devotion to victims of violent crimes.

"This is my car." She stopped at her sage-green Jeep Renegade.

"I'll call you when I have an office set up," he said.

This felt like the end of a really good date, connecting on a more personal level than they had ever before. She wondered if he felt it, too. He stood a little close to her, just outside the driver's side door. His blue eyes sort of twinkled as he took in her face.

"Okay," she said at last, looking at his lips.

When she lifted her eyes, she saw his flare with unmistakable desire. Hot tingles spread through her in instant response. Flustered, she dug in her purse for her keys and dropped them when she lifted them out.

He bent at the same time and their heads bonked.

Laughing and holding her head, she let him pick up her keys, hearing his deep chuckle. He unlocked her door and opened it for her.

Holding out her hand, she waited for him to drop

her keys there. He did, his rougher fingers brushing hers and stirring more hot tingles.

She climbed into her Jeep and he shut her door. She looked at him through the glass, watching him back up and then step onto the sidewalk, then started the engine, needing to catch her breath.

As she backed out of the parking space and began to drive away, she wondered what had just happened. Why him and why now?

She didn't have an answer, but she began to look forward to his call. Then she remembered her husband.

Chapter 2

"So, the Ice Queen isn't as icy as you thought."

Cal glanced over at Roman Cooper, who had finished moving his things into his office next to Cal's at Dark Alley Investigations. He wished he hadn't told him about the drastic change in Jaslene.

"No. We ended up having a great time." Cal shook his head. "She was a completely different woman."

"She liked the news of you coming over to DAI, huh?"

"Maybe that's all she liked. She hired me."

Roman chuckled. "Don't take it too hard. My bet is she's like you and something happened to make her turn away from love."

Had he turned away from love or just accepted that in his line of work it would take a rare woman to stick it out with him?

The front door opened and Jaslene appeared, wearing black slacks and a white-and-black-patterned blouse with a V-neck. Dressier than the last time he'd seen her, than any other time he'd seen her. Maybe something other than new hope for progress in the Everett case had changed her perspective. Had she worn this for him? While excitement over what could come zinged him, he held on to caution.

Someday, though, he'd like to see her in a little black number.

She looked around the new DAI office. He and Roman had rented a small space on Main Street, in the middle of a row of old, connected commercial spaces. It had a single door and window in front with room for a table where they could meet with clients. Two doors in back led to their offices and a hallway between led to a door that opened to a dark, creepy alley. They planned to do some upgrades but it would do for now.

As Jaslene approached Cal, he sensed her walls had gone back up. She didn't smile and he saw none of the sparkle that had been there a few days ago. Did she mean to keep this professional? They had started to get pretty personal.

"Come on into my office," he said, seeing Roman watching, an amused upward tilt to his mouth.

She followed him and he closed the door, ignoring Roman's mock shiver and rubbing of his arms. Ice Queen. Except Cal didn't think she was icy anymore. When he had told her about his grandfather, her sincere sympathy had touched him. He wondered what losses she had suffered to make her so compassionate.

Jaslene sat on the only chair before his desk. His bookshelf and desk took up most of the space.

"Have you made any progress?" she asked.

So they were back to that, with her barking at him to get things done. She may have dressed for him but she was in attack mode. Good thing he had news for her. Potentially big news.

"As a matter of fact…" He leaned to one side of his desk and found a report he'd printed yesterday. "Remember when I had Payton's house searched?"

"Yes."

"Well, I didn't tell anyone that I thought it had already *been* searched."

Her brows lowered. "Why not? That seems like an important detail."

"It is."

"Why didn't you tell anyone? Why didn't you tell me?"

"I wanted to be sure first. I also didn't want the press to leak it out." He felt like asking her if she remembered when he almost kissed her at her Jeep the other day.

"Oh." Her brow smoothed. "What is that?" She indicated the report.

"This is what Forensics recovered from Payton's computer. I asked them to do a deeper dive to search for evidence." He put it in front of her. "There were several emails deleted from her inbox, including some from her sent and trash folders. Forensics was able to recover enough to show Payton was in contact with a man named John Benjamin."

"She never told me about anyone named John."

Payton had kept it secret that she'd been corresponding with a man? Why? Why hide that, especially from her closest friend?

"Then it's possible she was the one who deleted everything."

Jaslene shook her head. "Why not just delete her received messages from her inbox? She must have had a reason she didn't tell me, or anyone, about him."

"And maybe that reason got her killed?"

She nodded, reading the report.

"John Benjamin is a local physician," Cal said. "A *married* physician."

Jaslene looked up sharply from the report. "Payton was seeing a married man?"

"It's hard to say what the nature of their relationship was, but it was more personal than a doctor-patient relationship. Go to the third page."

She did and he let her have time to read the email correspondence. Payton had started the chain by thanking him for lunch and saying they should do that again sometime. The doctor responded with an offer for dinner and Payton had agreed. The doctor said he would call her.

"They made arrangements to meet," she said.

"Yes. We just don't know why."

"If she was seeing a married man, I can see why she didn't tell me about him. It must have bothered her." Her eyes widened. "Do you think he may have killed her because she planned to tell his wife?"

"Like I said, hard to say. Dr. Benjamin is quite successful. He owns several medical clinics, one here in

Chesterville where he has an office, and in other states. He's a family doctor and employs home health care providers. He's got two kids and lives in a large home in Riverbend, one of Chesterville's most prestigious neighborhoods. His house would probably sell for over a million."

"Was Payton having an affair with a rich doctor?"

"It may not have been sexual." Cal stood and took his suit jacket from the back of his chair and put it on. "Let's start with a conversation with him. See what he says."

Dr. Benjamin's local office building was large and recently constructed. Jaslene walked inside when Cal opened the door for her. She tried not to react the way she had the other day, but every time he did something chivalrous like that she suffered an onslaught of warm-to-hot tingles. She did, however, manage to not let him know with any visible shiver or glance. She needed to keep this all business.

They were told the doctor was with a patient and waited. After thirty minutes, a nurse came out and called Cal's name.

Dr. Benjamin sat at his desk, working on his computer. He had thick, brown hair cut neat and short and hazel eyes, probably in his late forties, maybe early fifties and in good shape. He was handsome enough, but Jaslene failed to see what could have attracted Payton to a man like him.

He stood, allowing Jaslene to see he wore dark gray slacks and was about six feet tall. "My nurse said this was urgent. You're from where?" he asked. "Some kind of investigation agency?"

"Cal Chelsey. Dark Alley Investigations." He reached out his hand.

The doctor took it. "What's Dark Alley Investigations?"

Cal removed his wallet and took out a business card, handing that over. "It's an independent investigations agency that specializes in cold cases."

He turned to Jaslene and lifted her hand. "And you are?"

"Jaslene Chabot."

"A pleasure to be sure." He kissed the top of her hand. "What is a beautiful woman like you doing with a private detective?"

Jaslene pulled her hand away. His charms might work on some women but not her.

"I'm investigating Payton Everett's disappearance. Jaslene was one of her close friends."

"Payton? She is a patient of mine." The doctor's gaze shifted to Cal and his brow wrinkled. "I'm sorry. I don't understand."

"When is the last time you spoke with or saw her?" Cal asked.

The doctor thought a moment. "Gosh. It's been months. I don't recall exactly. I could have my receptionist check."

"Is the only time you saw her when she came in for appointments?"

"Yes."

"So, you're saying you never met her for lunch or dinner?"

"Met her?"

He had to be acting. Payton had thanked him for lunch and he'd invited her for dinner. Had he called her? Had another meal taken place?

"I had a forensics team take a look at Payton's computer and we found several emails had been deleted from all the folders in her account."

Jaslene noticed how Cal waited for any kind of reaction from the doctor. She didn't see any. He looked confused.

"The emails that were deleted were correspondence between you and Payton. You had lunch with her and made arrangements to meet her for dinner."

The doctor lifted his head as though something finally dawned on him. "Ah. Yes. I did meet her for lunch. She needed a chiropractor, so I planned to introduce her to one."

Jaslene remembered Payton had mentioned wanting to find a chiropractor, though she hadn't mentioned what doctor she was seeing or that she'd met him.

"The chiropractor couldn't make it, though."

"So it was just you and Payton," Cal said.

"Yes."

"Were you having an affair with her?" Jaslene asked.

The doctor turned to her. "I'm married."

"That's why I called it an affair."

"I could lose my medical license having affairs with patients."

He hadn't really answered the question. Was he avoiding the truth? Or had he just admitted to an affair by way of omission?

"Did you see her again after you had lunch?" Cal asked.

"I don't remember. I don't think so."

He didn't remember? Jaslene didn't believe him.

"Did you meet her outside the office any other time before that?" Cal asked.

The doctor hesitated. "You said Payton has been missing?"

"Yes. For seven months now."

"I didn't know." His head lowered as though he fell into thought. "She is a lovely woman. I enjoyed our friendship."

"You were friends?" Cal asked.

"Not close. Otherwise I'd have known she went missing, wouldn't I?"

"One would think," Cal said. "Do you always meet patients outside your clinic?"

"Not always. Payton didn't have time to drive to the clinic so I told her I'd meet her. That's when we had lunch."

"Did you meet her any other times or for any other reasons?" Cal asked again.

Jaslene wondered if Cal was trying to fool him into answering or catch him in a lie.

"Are you asking me these questions because you think I had something to do with her disappearance?"

"Did you?" Cal asked.

"No. If the police want to question me, then they

can. As far as I can see, I don't have to answer any of yours."

Clearly they would get nowhere with this man. Why had he initially denied meeting Payton?

Cal opened the door for Jaslene as they left the medical building, seeing how she flashed a glance at him as she passed. The side of her breast brushed his arm and her gaze turned smoky. He felt his own reaction to that, an ignition of desire he had to quickly squash.

"What do you think?" she asked as they walked toward his SUV.

"That it's strange he met Payton outside of the clinic and didn't have an affair with her." And that he was so evasive about meeting her at all.

"And that he wouldn't say whether he met Payton outside the office more than once."

He glanced at her with a nod. She had echoed his next thought. "Yes, that, too." Did he not admit to an affair to protect his marriage? Had neither told anyone about it or had there really been no affair? Even if they had, keeping it secret didn't mean he killed her. He also could have been evasive for the same reason—to protect his marriage.

"Payton isn't the kind of woman who'd tell her lover's wife," Jaslene said. "She wouldn't threaten to, either. I'd be more inclined to believe she was the one who ended the relationship because it was wrong."

"If there *was* an affair."

"There had to have been. Why else would he have skirted around the questions?" she asked.

"I'm leaning toward affair as well, but he may not have anything to do with Payton's disappearance. He may only want to protect his marriage." Cal was on the fence as to whether his sense of suspicion held any merit.

"How far would he go to do that?" She stopped walking all of a sudden.

Cal followed her gaze to a man sitting in an old Ford pickup, smoking a cigarette and watching them. He wore a baseball hat over brown hair and Cal knew from the files he had read that his eyes were also brown. He was five-ten and a scrawny hundred and seventy-five pounds.

Riley Sawyer.

"I saw him about a month ago. He was standing on the sidewalk in front of my house."

"Watching you?"

She nodded. "I threatened to call the police and he left, but not before telling me it was my fault Payton was dead. He said if I hadn't interfered, they would still be together and she would have never been kidnapped."

"Why didn't you tell me?"

Jaslene turned to look at him. "I only saw him that one time."

"But he threatened you."

"He's not the sharpest cheese in the deli. He was always overreacting when he was with Payton. I thought it was a onetime thing and he was eliminated as a suspect. If I saw him again, I would have told you."

"If anything happens that seems off, no matter how insignificant it is, tell me."

She nodded. "He blamed me for Payton's death. That means he's upset she's gone. Why would he kill her?"

"Why does anyone kill? He might have realized he would never have her again and then decided he had to make sure no one else would, either. He may have killed her in the heat of passion. Maybe he didn't mean to."

He saw Jaslene consider that as her expression turned graver. Riley puffed on his cigarette, still calmly watching them. What a creepoid.

She rubbed her arm as though chilled.

Riley threw out his cigarette and formed a gun with his hand, pulling an imaginary trigger as he aimed at Jaslene.

Jaslene inhaled. "Did he just…"

Incensed that the man would dare to make such a gesture, Cal started walking toward him. Riley pulled out onto the street and vanished into traffic.

Returning to Jaslene, he put his hand on her lower back and guided her toward his SUV.

"We'll take another look at his alibi."

She didn't respond but he felt her lean a little closer to him. "Doesn't it scare you to chase after people like that?"

He opened the passenger door for her but she didn't get in. She faced him.

"No. It was a bit of an adrenaline rush at first but I got used to it."

"In Texas? What did you do there?"

"I joined the army reserves. Did that part-time while

I went to college for criminal justice. After that I was a state trooper for a few years before I became a ranger."

"And then you came here?"

"Hop in." He didn't feel like talking about that right now. Not only was it too personal, it also dredged up memories he didn't want in his head.

She eyed him peculiarly before climbing up into the SUV. He walked around the front and got in beside her, starting the engine.

"Why here?" she asked. "You could go anywhere to get away from your family. Why Chesterville?"

"My ex-wife's family lives here."

A heavy silence passed. With a sigh, Cal didn't pull out into traffic. Now she'd be too curious to let it go. That was another bad memory he didn't want cluttering his head.

"You were married?" she asked.

"Divorced. Two years ago."

"Oh."

Was he mistaken or did she sound relieved? He looked at her. With her head bent and hands in her lap, she seemed sad. Why?

"Are you all right?"

"I was married, too," she said quietly.

"Did you have as much fun with your divorce as I did with mine?" he asked, his voice full of sarcasm.

"I wasn't divorced. My husband was shot during a road rage incident. Also two years ago."

Cal felt like an ass. "I'm sorry."

"Two other drivers were driving erratically. My husband was on his way home from work and was caught between them. The one with the gun passed my husband's car on the passenger side and the other road rager passed him on the driver's side. The shooter shot and hit Ryan."

That was terrible. She must still be heartbroken. Roman had them both pegged. Something had happened to make Jaslene shy away from love, just like him. She had a bigger reason. How devoted was she to her late husband?

She had to be dealing with some serious grief, or had over the last two years. And now she would likely have to bury another person she loved.

"Jaslene, you should prepare yourself for not finding Payton alive. In most cases when a victim is missing this long, we're looking for a body, not a live person."

She met his gaze unhappily. "I know."

He reached over and put his hand on hers, taking it and giving her a supportive squeeze. She smiled, still sadly, but he could tell his action touched her. It had been a long time since he'd connected with anyone, a woman. Betrayal had made him withdraw from getting too personal.

"Talking to that doctor made me realize something."

"What?" What could a doctor, a stranger, have to say that would give her an epiphany?

"If he did have an affair with Payton, it wasn't planned. Payton wouldn't have gotten involved with a married man if she could have avoided falling for him. And Dr. Benjamin seems like a nice person. He didn't get insulted when we asked him about an affair."

"He has a good bedside manner." A man like that could fool a lot of women.

"But I can see how it could happen. I *know* how it can happen."

She turned her head and looked out the window, putting her hand to her mouth. He could feel her tension.

"What do you mean you know?" He began to get a bad feeling about this. Did she have something else she'd kept hidden, like the good doctor had?

"Before my husband was killed…"

He predicted what she would say and everything in him went rigid.

"Let me guess…you had an affair." Just when he thought he'd connected with another woman she turned around and revealed she was no different from his ex-wife. That's why he didn't date much. He didn't trust women. He preferred to have solid confidence that his significant other wasn't the type to sneak around with other men.

She looked at him. "It's not what you think."

He yanked the gear into Reverse and backed out onto the street. "It never is."

"Why are you so mad?"

"Thanks for being so honest. I do appreciate that." He couldn't help snapping at her as he drove down the street.

"Wha— How dare you!"

"How dare I? You're the one who cheated on her husband right before he got himself shot to death. Did he know?"

Her mouth had dropped open.

"Did he?"

"No."

What was that old saying? Once a cheater, always a cheater? Cal would be sure to steer wide and clear of this one.

"I didn't cheat," she said. "Not really."

He wanted to ask her what her definition of "not really" was. "Did you kiss him?"

Her lack of reply gave him the answer he needed.

"Why are you so mad? I didn't do anything wrong."

"That's exactly what my wife said when I read her text messages with another man."

"Ah." Jaslene nodded. "That's why you were divorced. Your wife cheated and now you think every woman is the same."

"Not every woman. Only the ones who *cheat*."

She gaped at him again. He could feel her anger and outrage and wondered why. How could she find herself faultless?

"You don't even know what happened."

He didn't need to.

"My wife tried to tell me her excuses, too. I didn't want to hear any details. After I found the texts, I followed her. What I saw with my own eyes was plenty."

"You saw them…naked?"

"No. I saw them start to get undressed in a bedroom. *His* bedroom. When I confronted her later, she denied it until I threw the text messages in her face and told her I saw her. Then she admitted it. I left and filed for a divorce the next day."

"Wow. You are bitter."

"Wouldn't you be?" Cal didn't even like thinking his ex-wife's name. She was just his past now.

After several seconds she said quietly, "Yes." And then after additional seconds, she added, "But I wouldn't be so quick to judge others who once found themselves in awkward situations."

He didn't respond. He didn't want to hear her side of the story. The only side he'd like to hear was her husband's, but he was dead and didn't even know his wife had been unfaithful. Still, there was something in the way she'd said she hadn't done anything wrong. Did she mean because she hadn't slept with another man, only kissed him? He didn't care. She'd said it herself: she'd found herself in an awkward situation and didn't have enough respect for the man she married to stop things from escalating. Bitter? Oh, yeah. He was bitter, all right. Every time he met a woman like Jaslene, someone he might be able to get intimate with, he was reminded of the pain he had suffered.

Cal had made himself a promise that if he ever found another woman, he could trust he'd be sure of two things. One, she would need to handle his work schedule; and two, he wouldn't choose someone who would ever cheat. He'd stay true to that promise. He'd rather be alone than risk that kind of betrayal again. Funny, before he'd caught his former wife with another man, he never imagined how much it would bother him. He supposed no one did...until it happened to them.

That's what Jaslene didn't understand. She didn't

realize the consequences of immoral, disrespectful decisions, what they did to those closest, to the one they married and once claimed to love.

Cal had realized something about himself, thanks to his ex-wife. Honor and integrity, *the truth*, were far more important to him than love. These feelings of attraction he had for Jaslene had to stop. He could never get involved with a woman like her.

Chapter 3

The next day, Jaslene put one harness boot down onto the slushy pavement and alighted from Cal's SUV. She couldn't look at him without anger flaring. She didn't tell him what happened in her awkward situation because he had labeled her without having the facts.

"I'll be back in about an hour," he said.

She turned back to see his handsome face, dark hair neatly trimmed and blue eyes glowing even on this dreary day. Irritation joined her temper. Why on earth was he still so attractive to her?

"Okay." She hated how attracted she was to him, a man who was so quick to judge.

Shutting the door harder than necessary, she ducked her head from the spitting snow and hurried into Pinocchio's. The hostess led her to where Catherine and Tatum already sat at a tall bistro table along the front window.

"Sorry I'm late." She sat on a chair next to the window, feeling a chill radiating through the glass.

"Who's the hottie?" Tatum asked, as Cal pulled out into a break in traffic, windshield wipers swiping big snowflakes clear.

Jaslene watched him disappear up the road, his profile blurred by moisture on the windows of the car and the restaurant, but still managing to imprint on her brain.

"Detective Chelsey," she said tersely, hanging her purse on the back of the chair.

"The detective you've been complaining about?" Catherine asked.

Jaslene shrugged out of her long black jacket and let it fall over the back of the chair, wishing they wouldn't go there.

"You're kind of edgy," Tatum said. "Is he still going nowhere with the case?"

"He dropped her off for lunch," Catherine pointed out. "They've been getting close."

Tatum observed Jaslene, scrutinizing her. "Have you?"

"You look nice today," Catherine said.

"She does," Tatum added.

"Would you two stop?" Jaslene had worn a long black sweater over heavy tights, nothing sexy but she wouldn't admit she'd taken more care getting ready today than she usually did. She wanted to make Cal squirm somehow for the things he had said to her.

"What happened to you?" Catherine asked with a sly smile.

"Nothing. What do you mean?"

"You haven't had a single nice thing to say about that detective and now he's dropping you off for lunch?" Catherine said. "Where were you before that? Obviously you were with him."

"I was at his new office. He left the force to join a private detective agency."

"Ooh, a man of action." Tatum fanned herself. "Apparently, he's not the slacker you had him made out to be."

"I never thought he was a slacker." Jaslene looked for a waitress, eager to get on with this before her friends exaggerated her relationship with Cal. Just because he dropped her off didn't mean there was something romantic going on between them.

"Not smart, then," Catherine said.

"No, I never thought that, either." She had always thought he was shrewdly intelligent. "He just seemed to…not care very much, or…not have any feelings about anything, really. But he quit the force because his boss was going to reassign him."

Tatum drew her head back and Catherine froze as she lifted her water glass.

"Wow. He…*quit his job* for you?" Tatum asked.

"No, not for me. To investigate freely." Her annoyance came out in her tone.

Tatum looked at Catherine at the same time Catherine looked at her, and then they both returned skeptical gazes to Jaslene.

"He only cares about the victims. He said so himself," Jaslene said.

"Did you have sex with him?" Tatum asked.

The question stunned her. "No!" How could they ask such a thing? She hadn't thought about sex with another man since before her husband died. She had felt the urge in her awkward situation and felt guilty about that to this day. But Cal had no right to judge her.

"I thought he wasn't doing anything to solve Payton's missing person case," Catherine said. She was always so practical.

"I thought he wasn't, either, but it turns out he was. He found evidence Payton's house and laptop might have been searched before police got there."

"My, oh my, he *is* smart," Catherine gushed.

The waitress came to deliver Jaslene a water. She hadn't even looked at the menu yet.

"Was anything missing that police didn't notice?" Tatum asked.

"I don't think so, but Payton was in contact with a man she never told me about. Did she ever mention she was seeing anyone to you?"

Tatum shook her head.

"No," Catherine said. "Did your detective find out she was?"

"We know she met a Dr. John Benjamin for lunch one day. He denies having any relationship with her and says she was his patient, but I can't get past how odd it is that she met him for lunch. He claims it was to introduce her to a chiropractor, but the chiropractor never showed up."

"I agree it's odd she met her doctor for lunch."

"She would have told us if she was seeing anyone," Catherine said.

"Dr. Benjamin is married." Jaslene waited for that to sink in.

Tatum drew her head back in surprise and Catherine just stared at Jaslene.

"Payton was having an affair with a married man?" Catherine said. "That is so not like her."

"I know," Jaslene agreed. "I think that's why she didn't tell us."

"Wait a minute." Tatum leaned forward on her elbows. "You're not saying you think the doctor kidnapped her and maybe killed her, are you?"

"What if Payton threatened to tell his wife?" Jaslene wanted to hear what her friends would say. "Maybe he told her he would leave his wife and then she found out he had no intention of doing it."

Catherine shook her head this time. "She wouldn't do that."

Jaslene didn't think so, either, but she'd wanted to know what they both thought.

"There's something else," Jaslene said. "I saw Riley the other day. He made a pistol with his hands and mimicked shooting me."

"Oh, that slithering snake." Catherine made a face.

"Why is Riley stalking you *now*?" Tatum asked.

"Did you tell the police?"

"Cal knows. I saw him outside my house a month ago, too. I've seen him around town, just random run-ins, like normal. But he stops and watches me, like he used to do to Payton. He's never made shooting gestures to me before. I guarantee you, I'd have told the cops if he did. There's nothing anyone can do about a man who's doing what he normally does in town and happens to run into me."

"He'd like to kill you," Catherine said. "Isn't that what his little gesture means?"

"That's how I took it," Jaslene said. "He had an alibi, but Cal is going to look into that again."

"It makes more sense that Riley had something to do with Payton's disappearance than a married doctor she might have been experimenting with sexually," Catherine said.

"Cal?" Tatum queried. "You just called your detective 'Cal.'"

"Detective Chelsey."

"You're calling each other by first names now?" Tatum teased. "Ooh la la." She wiggled her eyebrows suggestively.

"Stop it." Her friends knew her well enough to pick up on undercurrents.

"What's been going on between the two of you?" Tatum asked.

"Nothing." Her response, if she was truthful, would be wild attraction—before he had insulted her, but she would rather not go there.

Both Catherine and Tatum pinned her with doubtful gazes.

"Nothing," she repeated.

Tatum cocked her head dubiously and Catherine started to smile.

"Nothing is going on," Jaslene almost snapped.

"He's very good-looking," Tatum said.

"And manly," Catherine added. She'd married a tall man herself.

"There's nothing going on between us," Jaslene insisted. "In fact, I told him about Ansel and he assumed I cheated on my husband."

"You almost did," Tatum said.

Jaslene lowered her head with the pang of grief and regret that fact instilled. She felt like she had cheated. And Cal was right. Her husband had died not knowing the truth.

Tatum reached over and put her hand over Jaslene's. "I'm sorry. I know what a sensitive subject that is for you."

"You didn't cheat on Ryan," Catherine said. "Ansel kissed *you*. You didn't kiss *him*. You didn't do anything wrong."

Jaslene wished her heart would believe that. True, she hadn't been the one to initiate the kiss, but what it had made her feel was the part that felt wrong.

"I asked my husband what he would do if something like that happened to me," Catherine said. "He told me he'd beat the hell out of the man and make sure I felt loved." She smiled, full of affection for her man.

Had Jaslene's husband made her feel loved? Ryan had been a geologist like her. They'd gone to school together. Sometimes she thought both of them having the same profession wasn't such a good thing. They'd both had different ideas on certain earth processes, for one. For example, he supported global warming and had conviction that would be the cause of an apocalypse. She agreed humans were responsible for climate change, but she also thought the earth was far more powerful than any human influence. People would heat up the earth, but that didn't mean the planet would come to an end. The earth would recover, even if humanity did not.

She and Ryan had argued often. Jaslene had fallen in love with his intelligent mind and his dark good looks. Best friends, they'd shared a love of nature. But had that been enough? Why had another man sent sparks, which she had never felt with Ryan, chasing through her? She had liked Ryan's lovemaking and his kisses. But she hadn't been transported to outer space. She wasn't sure Ansel could have done that, either, but he had gotten off to a good start with that kiss.

"Well, you aren't a cheater," Tatum said. "You have integrity and respect for others. You don't have it in you."

"Tell that to Cal." Jaslene smiled to cover the sick feeling churning her stomach.

"Something tells me he's going to discover that on his own," Catherine said. "He doesn't know what he has yet."

What did he have? Her? Not yet, and Jaslene wasn't sure she ever wanted him to, since he thought so little of her now, without any details on what had really happened with Ansel.

Dr. Drake Faulkner, the chiropractor Benjamin had recommended for Payton, welcomed Cal into his office. He closed the door, muffling the sounds of voices considerably. Dr. Faulkner was almost six feet and fit, with salt-and-pepper hair and titanium glasses.

"Thanks for seeing me." Cal sat on a chair, taking in the stacks of files on the desk and cluttered windowsills. Outside, the snow had picked up, flakes hitting and melting against the glass.

"My receptionist told me it was important…related to a missing person who may have been a patient of mine?"

"Yes. Payton Everett."

The doctor's interest perked up. "She wasn't a patient of mine. She was referred to me but never came to see me. Seems I can't help you after all."

"I think maybe you can. What can you tell me about Dr. Benjamin?"

"What do you want to know?"

Rather than say he needed to know everything, Cal started with "Did he ask you to meet him and Payton for lunch?"

The doctor hesitated. "Yes, but I refused."

"You refused or didn't show up?"

The doctor leaned forward, elbows on the desk. "Mr. Chelsey, Dr. Benjamin asked me to meet with a potential patient. I found that ethically insulting, not to mention a risk to my practice."

"Why did you think it was ethically insulting?"

"Because I don't have personal relationships with my patients. If he intended to refer her to me, then why do it over lunch?"

"Why did Dr. Benjamin ask you to meet her?"

"Maybe he liked her. I don't know." Dr. Faulkner leaned back.

"What was the nature of your association with Benjamin?"

"I worked for him when I opened my practice, but I went out on my own because I didn't agree with his philosophy…like meeting patients for lunch."

Cal believed that. "Do you know if he had any kind of personal relationship with Payton beyond meeting her for lunch?"

"No. Like I said, she never came to see me and I went out on my own shortly after that incident." He tapped his fingers on the end of the armrest.

"If you worked for him, why the need for a referral?"

"His company is large and includes several clinics and practices. He had a referral program set up between them all."

He seemed agitated. "Why did Benjamin ask you to meet him and Payton for lunch? Why not just refer her to you like a normal doctor?"

Faulkner grunted derisively, his fingers stilling. "You just answered your own question, Mr. Chelsey. There's nothing normal about Dr. Benjamin. He's not a man who lives by any rules other than the ones he makes up himself."

A lot of criminals embarked on their wayward careers with that kind of mentality. Could Dr. Benjamin be behind Payton's disappearance? If he liked her as Dr. Faulkner suggested, that would be highly unlikely. Unless Payton posed a threat to him, but what threat could she pose? Telling his wife didn't seem enough for a motive. Maybe Faulkner just disliked the doctor.

"Can you tell me of any other incidents he caused?" Cal asked. "Do you think Dr Benjamin was having an affair with Payton?"

"It's possible. That wasn't the first time he took a patient to lunch, if that's what you mean. He had a way of treating his practice like it was a personal extension of himself. He grew a very successful business on charisma alone. He owns several clinics across the country now, including two home health care services companies. Many doctors and nurses work for those clinics. He's a multimillionaire. I give him credit for being smart, but I found his personal interactions with his patients too risky. I wanted no further association with him."

Dr. Benjamin did have a way of presenting himself as friendly. He had been kind and patient and cooperative up until the end, when he'd refused to answer any more questions. Jaslene had noticed that, too. But was that all a show?

"Did you remain in contact with Benjamin?" Cal asked.

Faulkner's fingers started tapping again. "No. He wasn't very happy with my decision to leave his company."

"Did he know why?"

"I didn't publicly condemn him for his ways. He wouldn't have liked losing the business. He lost most of my patients when I left."

"So, you were gone before Payton disappeared."

"Yes I was. I left shortly after he invited me to that lunch. I heard about Payton in the news."

"Do you think Dr. Benjamin could have been responsible for her disappearance?"

"I knew him but I didn't know him that well. I wouldn't make an assessment either way. I'm not even sure how involved he was with her."

He asked the chiropractor a few more questions about the day Payton disappeared, but he had already branched off on his own by then and had no contact with Benjamin or Payton for quite some time before that. He thanked him and left.

Time to go pick up Jaslene from her lunch with her friends. He wondered if she had cooled down yet, and part of him wanted to make it up to her.

Chapter 4

Jaslene looked at her cell phone again. Where the heck was Cal? Her friends had already left, Tatum on her way back to work and Catherine to run errands before she picked up the kids. Jaslene waited inside the doors of the restaurant, watching the wind pick up. The snowflakes had gotten heavier with the cooling temperature.

Movement across the street caught her eye. A small dog peeked out from behind a dumpster in an alley. The poor creature hung its head low and kept lifting its front paws. It was soaking wet.

Jaslene opened the restaurant door and walked to the edge of the street, waiting for traffic to pass before crossing. She reached the dumpster. The dog saw her and ducked behind the cold metal. She peered around the corner. It huddled against the wet brick of the building, shivering.

She saw now that it was a puppy, an adorable dog that looked like an Australian shepherd. It had no collar. Given its dirty, wet and shivering state, its must have been out here a while.

"Are you lost?"

The puppy lowered its head with a slight twitch of its ears.

Jaslene inched forward, crouching as she neared. "It's okay. I'm not going to hurt you."

The puppy lifted its head and Jaslene found herself looking into the saddest, most dejected eyes she'd ever seen, beautiful golden eyes that matched the two patches of eyebrows above.

"Oh, you poor baby." She touched the dog's wet, cold head and began petting it. "I'm going to get you warm and dry, okay?"

The puppy whimpered as a violent shiver racked the tiny body.

Jaslene choked back the sting of tears. "How did you get out here?" She gently lifted the dog, seeing it was a girl, parting her jacket and tucking her inside.

"Did you run off or did someone leave you?"

The puppy clung to her for warmth, whimpering more. Jaslene wrapped her jacket around the dog, feeling wetness seep into her sweater.

Going back to the street, she looked up and down the sidewalk and across the street. She saw no one out searching for a lost dog and saw no lost dog posters.

Cal's SUV pulled up to the restaurant. Jaslene hurried across the street, jogging in front of the vehicle to the other side.

She got in and the puppy clawed at her, trying to crawl closer. Tiny, precious whimpers accompanied grunts, piercing Jaslene with protective instinct.

"Is that a dog?" Cal sounded incredulous, as though he asked a question to which he already knew the answer.

"I found her in the alley."

After continuing to gape at her for several seconds, Cal started driving. "Doesn't it belong to someone?"

"Who would leave their dog out in this weather? Especially a puppy?" Even if the animal did belong to someone, she wasn't sure she'd give her back to anyone that heartless or careless.

"Do you want me to drive to the pound?"

Jaslene looked at him, appalled. "Is that what you would do? Dump a helpless puppy off at an animal shelter? She's obviously been through enough already." Jaslene pet the dog and kissed her drying head. She wasn't sure what she would do with the puppy yet, but she sure wasn't going to abandon the animal.

"An animal shelter will feel like home compared to an alley."

"Let's stop at the pet store on the way back to my place."

She spotted one just ahead.

"What if you get attached?" Cal asked as they walked toward the pet store.

Jaslene kept the puppy tucked in her jacket. "Then I'll keep her."

"Are you ready to take on a dog? You're going to decide on the fly to keep it?"

"She needs a home."

"The pound will find her one. Everybody loves puppies. It wouldn't take long for someone to pick her up."

Ignoring him, she entered the store and found a cart. As she lifted the puppy and put her into the front, the animal whimpered and tried to climb back up onto her.

"It's okay." She pet the puppy's tiny head. "We're going to get you some necessities, little girl."

Jaslene pushed the cart toward the dog food, Cal trailing behind. "Do you not like dogs?"

"I like them. I'm just being practical. They're a big responsibility. They aren't like cats."

"Are you a cat man?" She glanced back. He did not strike her as one.

"No. I'm a never-home man."

Glancing at him, she wondered if he really meant that. His job probably kept him busy and away from home a lot, but surely he had time for meaningful relationships. He just barred himself from them because of his nasty divorce.

She chose some dry and canned food and put them in the cart. The puppy hung its paws over the baby seat backing, sniffing the bag. She picked out two dog beds and then a collar and leash. Cal helped her by finding dog food and water bowls and she picked out a brush and some shampoo.

"If you're going to have a puppy, you better get some toys."

"Good point. I might not have any shoes left if I

don't." She found the toy aisle. Cal seemed to be getting into this.

Grinning, he held up a stuffed squirrel squeaky toy with big eyes and floppy tail. When he squeezed the chest, it make a chirping sound like a real squirrel.

Jaslene laughed and put it in the baby seat with the puppy. She picked out a ball and another chew toy and headed for the checkout.

"What if you have to give the dog up?" Cal asked.

"Are you always this depressing?" She understood he was only being practical, but for now she only wanted to take care of a helpless puppy. Didn't he see that?

He chuckled. "You're spending a lot of money on a dog who probably belongs to someone else."

"I'll give notice to the animal shelter and post some found posters, but I doubt anyone will claim her. Look at the poor thing. She's obviously abandoned."

"Or lost. Dogs run off."

"There you go with all your cheer again."

"No, I'm just good at avoiding a broken heart."

Didn't he mean *another* broken heart?

Cal watched Jaslene dry off the softly crying puppy after its warm bath. The maternal way she cared for the creature touched a soft spot in him, one he wasn't prepared to have touched.

"What are you going to call her?"

"I don't know. Crybaby, if she doesn't stop that pitiful sound."

"She's probably tired." Jaslene had already fed her

and given her some water. She'd put one dog bed in the living room and the other in the bedroom.

Wrapping her in a soft throw, Jaslene cradled the puppy, who gave a few grunts and rested her chin at the bend of her arm with drooping eyes. After a few exhausted blinks, the puppy fell asleep.

"I think my heart just melted," Jaslene said.

"Just like holding a baby." Cal wished he hadn't let that thought slip. He'd watched mothers hold their babies and imagined his wife doing the same someday. But she had destroyed any dream of having that together.

"You've held a lot of babies?"

"No." He brushed a finger over the top of the puppy's head, careful not to wake her up. He hoped she wouldn't dwell on that topic.

"Nieces and nephews?"

"It was just a figure of speech." Please, make her stop.

"Do you want babies?"

And there it was. Cal felt opened up and exposed right now. He struggled to maintain aloofness.

"I did." Maybe he could use this to cool this attraction between them; letting her know how important having a family had once been to him should accomplish that. He wished he could still look forward to that, but doing so would only lead to devastation.

"But not anymore?"

"I should get going," he said shortly.

She looked at him a moment and then seemed to

allow him to back off. "All right. Let me put Rapunzel to bed and then I'll see you to the door."

Apparently, she'd decided on a name, but why did she want him to wait? Why didn't she just let him leave? Did she intend to try and get him to talk about why he no longer wanted kids?

An image of her holding a real baby—his baby— struck him and he had to forcibly chase it from his mind.

She took the puppy to her room, presumably to put it to bed. Feeling a little foolish for waiting, Cal went to stand by the entrance in her living room, an earthy, no-fuss room that was more functional than decorative.

Hearing her return, he faced her.

"Um…" She lifted her hand and ran her fingers through her golden hair.

"It's a short walk." He extended his arm toward her front door.

She breathed a brief laugh and lowered her hand. "I didn't ask you to wait for that. Um…"

He waited.

"I… I know it's probably none of my business, but…"

Yep, he was right. "I don't want kids because I wanted them with my wife, who showed me that some people don't mean what they say."

"Not all people."

"She had me convinced she was the only one for me."

"Maybe she didn't plan on meeting another man. Maybe she didn't intend on hurting you." She reached out her hands toward him. "Look at you. You're a handsome man. She must have thought she was lucky to have you."

"No. She thought *I* was lucky to have *her*."

The amount of himself he had put into that relationship gnawed at him. He felt like an idiot for not recognizing the signs, the most glaring being that she had not loved him.

Jaslene put her hands on her hips…sexy hips. The sight calmed him and drove negative thoughts about his ex-wife away.

"Well, if that's true, why did you marry her?" she asked.

"I thought I was lucky to have her."

"What was so special about her?"

That was an excellent question. "She was career driven and liked doing the same things I do. She also seemed impressed with what I did for a living and told me she wanted a family."

"Does she have one now? A family?"

He hated that his ex-wife *did* have a family now. His face must have showed his sentiment.

Her mouth formed an O and he heard the faintest "Oh." She touched his forearm. "Now I understand why you're so bitter."

He fought off a heated reaction to her touch—that all too welcoming heat. "I'm no longer a dreamer. People die. People kill. People sleep around and get divorced. That's not only the thing that turns me off about having a family. It's my profession, too. I'm hardly ever home."

She stepped closer, letting her hand fall from his

forearm. "Why did you think it could work with your ex-wife?"

He liked looking at her soft, blue eyes that were the color of a Caribbean island bay. "I believed her. She said she'd be there for the kids when I couldn't be. I don't want to bring children into a family destined for dysfunction."

"Not all marriages fail."

"They say fifty percent fail but I think that number is closer to eighty."

She put her forefinger on his chest. "Maybe you should try to get past your divorce."

He had an urge to slide his arm around her and give her a kiss she wouldn't forget. "I am past it." He would never make that mistake again.

"No, you aren't. You think every woman is as untrustworthy as your ex."

"Not every woman." Only the ones who *cheated*. He left that unspoken.

Rising up onto her toes, she said in a husky tone, "I didn't cheat."

He wasn't sure if she deliberately encouraged him or if her attraction led her, but he didn't question. He just slid his arm around her waist, pulled her against him and kissed her.

He felt her stiffen and heard her sharp indrawn breath. But if she felt the same fire as him, she'd go with him on this expedition. Sure enough, she relaxed against him and moved her lips with his.

Just before he lost all ability to listen to caution, he gently withdrew. Her sultry eyes nearly did him in and had him going back for more. He needed to shut this down or things would move too fast.

"You didn't cheat because you didn't have the chance," he said.

She blinked a few times and then as awareness of his words seeped through her passion, her brows lowered. "What?" She pushed his chest and he stepped back, letting her go. "You don't know anything about me."

He grinned. "I know you're a good kisser." With that he turned and went to the door.

He might have joked around and flirted with her, but as he left the house, his gut roiled. What if he was wrong about her? He didn't want to hear what happened with her alleged affair.

He approached his car and noticed a familiar truck parked across the street. An instant later he recognized Riley. Damn, that man was bold. He didn't seem to care that he was seen.

Concerned for Jaslene's safety, Cal walked to the side of the truck, even more surprised when Riley lowered the window instead of driving away.

"What are you doing here?" Cal asked.

"I was waiting for Jaslene to come out so I could talk to her."

That seemed more than a little odd. Why wait in his truck? Why not knock on the door? Maybe he just said that and just got his rocks off stalking Jaslene. The man must have psychological issues. "What do you want to talk to her about?"

"I want to know what she's going to do to make up for causing Payton's death."

Cal met his angry eyes without flinching or giving away any reaction to that startling comment. "How do you know she's dead?"

"She's gone. She'd be here if she was alive," he snapped.

Did he really blame Jaslene for Payton's supposed death? "You think she'd still be here if the two of you were still together?"

Riley narrowed his eyes. "She would still be with me if Jaslene hadn't interfered."

"I'm not going to argue with you about anything. If you continue to stalk Jaslene, I'm going to have you arrested."

Riley put his truck into gear. "She's going to pay for what she did, and so will you if you keep hanging around her."

"I'd like to see you try. You go within fifty feet of her and I'll come after you."

"She may as well have killed Payton herself."

"Don't come back here again." Cal looked into the cab of the truck, searching for anything suspicious. There was a lot of trash, as though Riley spent most of his time in there.

Riley shifted on the car seat and Cal spotted a pistol in his right hand. He held it under his thigh but Cal saw part of the grip.

He met the man's eyes. "Why the gun, Riley?"

Riley just sent him another angry look before driving off.

Cal ran to his SUV, got in, started the engine and flipped a hasty U-turn before going after the truck.

He followed Riley through town, seeing him look into the rearview mirror several times. He knew Cal was tailing him.

Riley sped into a turn and Cal followed, removing his gun and readying it to fire if Riley threatened him. He checked his speed. About thirty over the speed limit. This road led out of town. Once they reached the open highway, Riley sped up more. Cal easily kept up.

Riley slowed and spun into a three-sixty. Cal started to do the same as Riley began firing. Cal ducked and came up to fire back, hitting Riley's driver's side door.

Riley then drove back into town, all the way to a run-down bar called Harley's Tavern. Cal had investigated Riley's whereabouts the night of Payton's disappearance, and he'd been at this bar. Riley parked in the potholed lot, looking back at Cal.

Cal parked on the street and got out. Now that he was private he couldn't arrest Riley, but he could easily have that arranged. The man posed a clear threat to Jaslene. Cal would feel a lot better if he was in jail.

Going into the bar, Cal put his gun away and searched for Riley. Country music played from a jukebox. People played pool and sat at the bar drinking. Only one of the six tables was occupied by two heavily made-up women in leather pants and jackets.

"Where did that man who just entered go?" he asked the bartender.

A tall man with a slightly protruding stomach, light hazel eyes and a bald head, the bartender nodded toward the restrooms. Cal hurried to the hall, seeing the restrooms and a doorway leading to a back area. He raced to the back door. As he opened it, he heard the sound of a motorcycle. Running out into the alley, he saw Riley riding away. He'd parked a bike here? Or had he stolen it?

Back inside, he went to the bar. "Do you know that man who came through here?"

"Yeah. Riley Sawyer. Comes in regularly. What was his hurry? He in trouble again?"

"He's a person of interest."

The bartender sized him up. "You a cop?"

"I was. I'm a private investigator now."

"You cops came in here a while ago asking about him. This about that girl that went missing?" the bartender asked.

"Riley ain't been the same since then. She was his girlfriend," one of the men at the bar, his dark eyes droopy and his light brown hair greasy, said. He smelled like he hadn't washed his jeans in a couple of weeks and like most everyone else in the bar, wore a leather jacket.

"His girlfriend?"

"He never stops talking about her," the bartender said, wiping the bar in one area.

"She put a restraining order on him before she went missing," Cal said.

"He never mentioned that," the patron said.

"He has been acting bizarre lately." The bartender poured two beers and a waitress took them on a tray from the bar.

"Only lately?" Payton had gone missing months ago.

"He was upset she was gone," the patron said. "But he seems to have progressively gotten worse."

"Crazier," the bartender added. "Like running through here to get to his bike and you showing up with a gun. Strangest thing I've seen so far."

"Definitely the strangest," the patron said, drinking some beer.

"Why did he park a motorcycle in the back?" Cal asked.

"He keeps it here sometimes. Says he doesn't have room for it at his apartment."

More like he parked it there in case he needed to get away from someone. Like Cal. Well, Cal would have to put some pressure on the man. He looked around for the waitress who'd served Riley the night Payton disappeared and didn't see her.

"What about the waitress that served him the night Payton went missing?" Cal asked the bartender. "Where is she?"

"She doesn't work here anymore."

He supposed she had no reason to lie and decided to look for other clues.

"Thanks," he said to the men, then headed for the door, taking out his phone on the way.

He'd report what happened to the police. Nobody started shooting at him and got away with it. Nobody threatened someone under his protection, either. While he could not think of Jaslene as a victim, she could become one, if Riley had his way. He refused to allow that to happen. Normally he investigated victims who were already dead. Rarely did he have a chance to prevent a living one from being harmed.

Imagining anything terrible happening to Jaslene

gave him a sense of apprehension. He didn't think he would feel the same intensity with anyone else. With most cases, he'd have this usual ambition to see it through, but not with this much personal investment. That caused him some anxiety. Like thinking of her having and holding his baby, protecting her felt too intimate.

Chapter 5

The next morning, Jaslene handed Cal a few flyers featuring a picture of Rapunzel and her cell phone number. Found Lost Dog, the print said. She dreaded doing this. Especially now that she had named the sweet thing, she had grown attached, but she had to do the right thing and do all she could to find the dog's owner. Only Cal's nearness and the memory of him kissing her softened the task with distraction. Good thing she wore a pair of red gloves and couldn't feel his skin when he took the flyers. She wore a matching red scarf with her black jacket and also a hat and a pair of new snow boots. It was supposed to snow several inches today.

Jaslene adjusted her red scarf over her jacket.

He looked handsome in his winter jacket and jeans, with his thick hair waving in a slight breeze.

"Riley was outside your house when I left. I followed him to Harley's Tavern."

That revelation alarmed Jaslene. She had not noticed Riley outside her house. This was getting terrifying. He was aggressively stalking her.

"He got away on a motorcycle he parks behind the bar, but I talked with the bartender and a patron. They didn't reveal anything new, just shared some observations on how obsessed with Payton he was and how her death changed him."

Jaslene looked around for any sign of Riley. She didn't see his truck anywhere.

"I stopped by the station and talked with some friends. We studied the case again and they said they would be on the lookout for Riley."

He turned to a light pole and taped a flyer there. "What are you going to do if someone responds to these?"

Jaslene didn't like thinking about that. But she would do the right thing. "Give her back. I checked the My Neighborhood site for any postings on missing dogs and there were none," Jaslene said. "I also checked with the Humane Society and nothing turned up there, either. I have an appointment with a vet to check for a microchip and have her examined just in case."

"You could just keep the puppy." Cal looked at her, his tone teasing.

If she had lost a dog, she would want the person who found it to try to return it to her. The right thing to do was this, stapling or taping posters to light poles near where she'd found Rapunzel.

"Maybe no one will claim her."

"You shouldn't have named her."

"You saw her, would not naming her have been any different?"

He chuckled. "Probably not."

The deep sound of his laugh fanned her senses. She stapled a poster to a light pole.

"We did something similar for Payton," Jaslene said. "Not to compare humans to dogs. We searched a lot harder for Payton."

She'd hoped something would come of the effort but nothing ever did.

They walked down the sidewalk, snow beginning to fall from low gray clouds. She could see her breath, and Cal's. The heart of Chesterville had the charm of a Dickensian village. New this year were the strings of white lights hanging across the street between the town's oldest buildings. Black metal lampposts and large stone planters that held bursts of color in summer lined the entire stretch of buildings for three blocks. Awnings covered the entry of many stores. Signs hung above entrances, some extending out on brackets. Umbrellas from the patios of cafés and pubs had all been taken in for the winter.

She glanced at Cal, amazed yet again by his kindness. He didn't have to come out here and help her today. His job was to find Payton, but what would his next steps be?

"I know you checked all her coworkers, but did you look into the articles she reported?" Jaslene asked.

Payton had been an enthusiastic reporter for their small-town newspaper. Reporting took artistic talent as much as clever curiosity. Payton was smart like Jaslene. Where Jaslene thrived on hard science, Payton loved figuring out people and their interesting situations.

"Nothing stood out until we found out about Dr. Benjamin. After that I did some more checking. She did a small piece on him and his business."

"Can I see it?"

"Sure." He found it on his cell phone and showed it to her.

Stopping on the sidewalk in the middle of the town square, Jaslene held her stack of flyers in one arm and read a short article about Dr. John Benjamin held in her free hand. Other than Payton's crisp, witty writing, it was exactly as Cal described: a community section article on the success of Benjamin's company and the fortune of little Chesterville at having one of his clinics located here.

"How did the two of you meet?"

Jaslene handed him his phone back and felt an automatic smile spread from her mouth to her soul. "She moved here her sophomore year in high school. Her mother's family is from here and this is where they decided to retire when the time came." She recalled seeing her for the first time. In a small community like this, it was easy to spot newcomers. "Payton wasn't happy about the move. She left her friends and didn't know anyone her last year of school."

"That would be tough on any teenager."

She adjusted the remaining flyers to protect them from moisture. The snow had begun to pick up. "Her locker was next to mine. The minute I said hello and introduced myself I knew we were going to be friends. She cheered up when we started talking. Turns out our grandparents were good friends." Jaslene laughed lightly, the memory making her feel good. "We had math together and I discovered she had a knack for numbers and formulas like me. We studied together. After we graduated we planned to attend the same college. She said she wanted to be a writer."

"Writers are smart people."

Realizing she hadn't stopped smiling, she started walking again. Payton was probably gone. All she had were memories. "On campus, we lived in the dorm the first year, and then found a house to rent. We put an advertisement out to rent out the other two rooms so we could save money. Catherine and Tatum answered the advertisement. We all ended up becoming close friends through college." She glanced over at him as he walked beside her. "We weren't into partying like a lot of other students. We liked to go out and have a good time but we were all the same when it came to that. We all had dreams and college was part of those."

Cal chuckled. "I partied but didn't overdo it. And college was about more than getting good grades and launching a good career. It was also about women."

She sent him a teasing, openmouthed look of shock.

"We had our fair share of men," she said as she worked. "We didn't sleep with just anyone, though."

"Neither did I, but there were a few who passed the bar."

So he was experienced sexually. Was that what he intended her to think? He went to a nearby tree growing up from a square in the concrete to attach another flyer.

"Once I graduated and started working, reality set in," he said. "I got recklessness out of my system in college. And maybe a little rebellion after living under my father's iron fist."

They started walking again.

"Was he that bad?" Jaslene asked.

"He never laid a hand on any of us, but his temper could be triggered anytime someone disagreed with him." He glanced over at her, his breath fogging the chilly air. "Not the little things. Only things he held dear. He felt that everyone should make their own way in life, no matter the circumstances. If a person can breathe and blink their eyes, they can work." He stapled a flyer to another tree.

"Sounds like the two of you are just really different. You want to help people and your dad is more interested in success and making money." Jaslene figured she wouldn't care what profession a man had as long as he balanced work and home. She wondered if Cal was being fair. He spoke of all the negative things about his father and nothing good. A father couldn't produce a man like Cal and be all bad.

"Yes. Very different. He never donates to charity and wouldn't help anyone down on their luck. My brother is the same way. If anybody told me he was a clone of my father, I'd believe them."

She taped the last flyer to the light post at the end of the block. "What about your mom?"

"My dad adores her. I guess he respects her because she earns her keep working on the ranch. My sister is the most normal. My grandfather was the only one who ever understood me."

Jaslene didn't know what that would be like. Everyone in her family knew each other almost as well as they knew themselves. Cal must have obstacles to get over before he could resolve the issues he had with his family, mainly his father and brother. His divorce was a separate thing.

"What kind of ranch does your family run?"

"Mainly cattle, but they have lots of other animals."

She turned her face away from windblown snowflakes. A gust brought in a thick sheet of white. The weather forecast called for several inches today.

"Looks like the storm has set in." Cal took her hand and led her to a nearby pub.

Cal held the door for her and she stepped inside, stomping her feet and brushing snow off her hair. Country music played at an easy volume. A few people sat at a bar with backlit shelving containing numerous bottles of booze. Close to noon now, couples, groups and families occupied almost half of the long, narrow sea of square wood tables. Televisions hung in corners, on the long wall and above the bar. The smell of hamburgers reminded Jaslene she'd eaten an early breakfast. She'd been here once or twice before.

At a table by the front window, Jaslene removed her gloves, hat and scarf and stacked them out of the way on the table. Shrugging out of her jacket, she draped it over the back of the chair. Cal was already sitting, his azure-blue Henley bringing out the lighter color of his eyes. Taking the stool across from him, she watched it snow while they waited for their waitress. He ordered coffee and a mushroom and Swiss burger; she ordered tea and a regular cheeseburger.

"What's the wildest thing you've ever done?" Cal asked. "Besides the affair."

As the black sheep in his family, he likely had done quite a bit during his rebellious years. "I didn't have an affair," she snapped. "Stop saying that unless you know for a fact it was an affair."

He looked contrite. "Sorry. You still haven't told me what happened."

And she didn't feel like it now. "In truth, I must have been much more boring than you. I honored my parents' rule that we be home by ten. I got good grades in high school and college and I work hard as an adult. There really isn't much more to say."

"You didn't go cruising or car racing? No parties?"

"No cruising or racing. I went to football games and concerts. A few parties, but not many. I was more into prom and homecoming."

She saw his gaze travel down over the fitted long-sleeved button-up blouse. She had left the top three buttons undone.

"What about college?" he asked.

"Studied. Went out for dinner with the girls. Clubbing a few times, but only to go dancing. I made myself a promise that I wouldn't find my future husband in a bar." She'd met her husband in a calculus class. He'd been everything she thought she wanted in a man. Only after he was shot and killed did she begin to realize he may not have been. The man she had nearly had an affair with made her feel things she had never felt before, but she had always believed she married the love of her life and Ansel had not meant more than that. Being unfaithful went against everything she believed and honored. Then Ryan had died and after she had time to reflect, she realized she had not loved him as much as she thought.

Their drinks arrived and Jaslene warmed her hands around the teacup.

"I got good grades, too, but I also went to a lot of parties and bars. I hung with a rough group and never came home when my parents told me to."

He didn't have to say more. Outlooks and values conflicting with his father's distanced him from his family, but he hadn't lost sight of what he wanted in life. She doubted he had ever felt lost. Full of conviction, but never lost. Until his wife had an affair. She both resented his inability to put his experience with his ex-wife behind him and admired him for being such a righteous and caring man.

"What was your grandfather like?" She figured that would be the best way to get to know him better without being obvious that she was prying.

Cal's face lightened and she could feel the love he felt for the man. "He was a coal miner who smoked and drank whiskey. He never overdid it, though. He enjoyed people of all kinds. It didn't matter what color their skin was or what standing they had in society. Everyone was equal in his eyes—equal in the sense that no one was better than anyone else. What he enjoyed most in them was what made them different."

She let him stay in his memories, sensing he wasn't finished and enjoying the revelation that he took after his grandfather more than his father.

"He was more of a dad to me than my own." He looked out the window, where the snow fell heavier and slanted with the wind. "My dad worked all the time. I would go stay with Grandpa on weekends and breaks during school. We played cards and chess. He took me to football games. We fished and read books. He and my father argued all the time. They didn't get along and neither did I with my father. Grandpa said he raised my dad wrong. He was the best person in my life." The light in his face dimmed.

A tender spot warmed and blossomed, compelling her to put her hand over his. "When did he die?"

"Right before I went to college."

"Did you meet your wife before or after he died?"

He sent her a perplexed look. "After."

So, he'd perhaps latched onto the wrong woman to fill a void. She slid her hand to her side of the table. He must have grieved terribly. The loneliness had probably torn him apart, although she doubted he'd ever admit that.

"I remember one time I had a fight with my dad over the usual. Later, my grandfather told me it doesn't matter what you do with your life, you just have to like it. If you want to be president, then go be one. If you want to be a janitor, then go be one. Just pick the right state so you can afford the cost of living." He grinned and laughed shortly, wryly. "My dad hated that." His bittersweet humor faded and he turned to look out the window.

Jaslene felt the deep love he had for his grandfather. She also felt the equally penetrating loss. How sad that the most important man in his formative years had died.

Dishes clanked and people talked around them. Waitresses delivered orders. A busboy cleared the table next to theirs. A cool draft of air radiated off the window.

Turning back to Cal, she saw he'd returned from his view of the street. Their eyes met and a moment of warmth passed between them. Talking about his grandfather helped open him up, whether he'd anticipated that or not.

"When's the last time you spoke with your father?" she asked.

"Other than Christmas? Years. Three. He doesn't call so he must not miss me. No one in my family calls."

They were too busy making money, working. At least, that's what she imagined Cal would say.

"Maybe they think you don't want them to call."

"Trust me, they don't want to talk to me. They know I don't agree with their way of living."

"But they're your family. Maybe you should agree to disagree."

He chuckled cynically. "Newman would never do that."

Newman must be his father. Cal clearly believed it was either his father's way or no way, but Jaslene didn't believe for a second that after all this time his father wouldn't want his own son in his life. And if she was wrong, then he deserved to never see or speak to his son again. Cal should at least be able to put any uncertainties to rest. He might sound certain when he said his family didn't want to talk to him, but he must have some kind of emotions on the matter. A person didn't walk away from their family without any scars.

"You should let your father know how you feel."

His brow lifted incredulously. "You mean I should call him up and tell him I'm glad he never calls because I can't stand the way he lives? That when I watched all my superhero cartoons as a kid I always thought the underdog represented me and the villain represented my father?"

"Yes." That was exactly what he should do. She had to stamp down the surge of affection his analogy instilled. He himself was an underdog, the champion of victims. "If he truly doesn't care, then when your conversation is over, none if it matters anyway."

"If he wants me in his life, then he can pick up the phone and call *me*."

He'd allow stubbornness to keep his family at a distance? "Everyone needs their parents to love them."

"That's coming from someone who has that love,

and I don't think you understand. You don't know what it's like to grow up with people who only care about themselves."

He wasn't ready to resolve that part of his life and she wasn't the one to enlighten him. She did feel he needed a lesson in love. She just wasn't sure she was up for that task. She had had a major loss of her own. She didn't think she wanted to be the one to teach him.

The next day, Cal drove them to Riley's apartment building and kept the SUV warm as they kept watch over Payton's stalker. The storm had passed and left in its wake cold temperatures.

He didn't feel like talking. What Jaslene had suggested, about calling his father, disturbed him. Cal did call on Christmas but his father never called on any occasion. Cal had to be the one to pick up the phone. He truly did believe his family would never miss him but what if Jaslene had a point? What if he told them what he thought and maybe they'd reach an agreement to disagree, as she said?

"He doesn't appear to be home," Jaslene said of Riley.

She was right. They'd arrived early enough to tail him if he drove to work. Cal had read from police reports that he worked as an IT vice president at a tech company. That explained how a man like him could attract a woman like Payton, or at least that's what he surmised Jaslene would say. She must like ambitious men. People didn't become VPs if they were the settling type.

Cal wasn't so sure Payton had very good judgment when it came to men. A few weeks ago, while still on the police force, Cal had spoken with the human resources director at West Virginia Tech. She revealed Riley was in a probationary period due to stalking Payton. He'd also been accused of sexual harassment at his previous place of employment and must have covered it up because the HR woman didn't know that.

Payton might also have gotten involved with a married man. Maybe there were things Jaslene didn't know about her friend.

"Do you think he left town?"

"He did shoot at me." If Riley had gone, he'd done so to avoid being arrested.

He took out his cell phone and called West Virginia Tech. After being transferred a few times, he finally got in touch with Riley's boss.

"He hasn't shown up for work in a couple of days. We tried to find him but can't. Do you know if anything's happened to him?" the director of IT said.

"No. We need to locate him for questioning in association with a missing persons case."

"You think he's involved in Payton's case?"

"We only need to speak with him. He's a person of interest, not a suspect."

"Well, he's been acting strange for months now. If he doesn't have a good reason for not showing up to work, I'm going to have to fire him."

"Has he expressed any feelings on Payton Everett?"

"He never mentioned anything to me but his coworker told me he's been upset over not being able to find her."

Riley was looking for Payton? Or had he only said that to throw off those around him?

"Did he talk about Jaslene Chabot?"

"His coworker didn't say."

Cal ended the call and disconnected.

"We could try his family," Jaslene said.

"Let's see if we can find anything inside his apartment. You should wait here."

"Your SUV is nice but my feet are freezing."

"Why didn't you say something? I can turn up the heat."

"They'll warm up if I move around." She opened the door and got out before he could tell her to stay.

They walked through the snow toward the upscale apartment building. Jaslene had dressed warmly in a black turtleneck with a coat that hung down past her sexy butt.

No cars or people moved. A few cars passed on the street, their exhaust fogging the air and tires crunching over packed snow. Leaving the parking lot, they climbed the stairs to the second floor and made it to Riley's apartment. Cal rang the bell.

When no one answered, he looked from one end of the hall to the other and then took out his picking tools.

"Isn't this illegal?" Jaslene asked.

"We won't take anything. This is information gathering only. I'll find a legal way later, if something turns up in here."

After several minutes he unlocked the door and stepped into the entry.

Cal checked all the rooms. Riley wasn't here, and in the master bedroom, the closet door was open and clothes lay strewn on the floor. A small piece of luggage lay open there as well. It looked like Riley had packed another suitcase in a hurry.

"In here," Jaslene called.

He found her in the second bedroom. She had a closet door open. Riley had removed the shelf and rod and tacked up pictures of Payton. The entire wall was covered with photos.

"I can't say this is surprising," Cal said.

"No." She pointed to empty spaces. "It looks like he took some of them with him."

Cal saw small holes where patches of wall were visible, indicating a tack had once held a photo. "Good eye."

Riley was on the run, whether he had planned it that way or not. He didn't care if Jaslene knew he was coming after her. Even more disturbing, Riley wasn't even afraid of Cal. Did he know anything about his background? Cal had sent his own message—Riley shouldn't threaten Jaslene and not expect retaliation.

Chapter 6

The following night, Jaslene and Cal entered Harley's where Cal had chased Riley and lost him. Taking in the well-weathered interior, she realized the stalker had a secret life. As an IT expert, he made a decent salary and yet hung out in Chesterville's only hole-in-the-wall bar. Cal used his extensive resources to uncover more about the man. He frequently flew to Las Vegas or drove to Summersville to gamble and regularly stopped at Harley's after work.

She followed Cal's tall form to the bar, trying not to keep looking at his butt in those black jeans whenever the puffer jacket rose up high enough as he moved. It seemed like a slow night, with only one man on a stool and two tables that held a raggedy, long-haired, bearded man, a woman in a dirty sweatshirt and two construction workers.

"You find Riley Sawyer?" the bartender asked. "He hasn't been in here since you were last here."

"Not yet. We'd like to talk to the waitress who served him the evening Payton Everett went missing. Sharon? Do you know where we can find her?"

The bartender paused in wiping the bartop. "I fired her. She drank on the job."

Jaslene didn't recall reading anything like that in any of the reports Cal let her read after he quit the force. "Was she drinking the night Riley was here?"

"Can't be sure. No one complained that night, but she drank every other evening, so probably so. Staff complained about her breath and having to cover her tables."

"Did you tell police?" Cal asked.

"Didn't see a reason to. You already questioned her."

Jaslene sent a look to Cal.

"We questioned several patrons," Cal said. "And I'm not with the police anymore."

"No one talked to me and I might have been here that night. I come here a lot."

Jaslene turned to the lone man at the end of the bar. Clean-shaven with wavy dark hair that hung to his shoulders, he seemed healthy and bright-eyed. If he drank a lot, he didn't show it.

"I heard about the missing girl but I didn't know the cops came here to question anyone," the man said.

She followed Cal down the bar. Cal sat to the man's right and she to his left.

He held out his hand to Cal. "Hewitt Sadira."

Cal shook his hand. "Cal Chelsey. This is Jaslene Chabot."

Hewitt shook her hand, his gaze lingering on her face, telling her he thought she was attractive.

"You know Riley Sawyer?" Cal asked.

"Not well, but I've sat with him at this bar a few times. When exactly did this girl go missing? Seems it's been a while, but what day?"

"The Friday before Memorial Day," Cal said.

"Weekend before?" Hewitt rubbed his chin as he thought. Then he nodded. "The weekend before Memorial Day, I had plans to go to Pennsylvania to visit my grandmother. She wasn't going to make it to Chesterville for Memorial Day because she just had a hip replacement. I remember coming here that Friday night. Riley was here."

"What time was he here?" Cal asked.

"Right after he got off work. Sat here and had two beers and left."

Jaslene met Cal's eyes.

Hewitt turned to her. "Is something wrong?"

"Sharon said he left after ten."

"You mean Sharon, who was fired for drinking on the job? She worked over by the windows that night." Hewitt glanced back to the now empty tables. "A guy who looked similar to Riley sat at one of them. He was alone."

And nobody had caught on to that? Jaslene remembered Cal told her Sharon had said the man at the table who might have looked like Riley had paid cash, so she could have mistaken him for Riley.

"Did Riley, or the man who looked like him, pay cash for his beers?" Jaslene asked.

"He always paid cash."

The bartender finished serving the waitress with a tray full of beers and then headed down the bar toward them.

"Did you see Riley sitting at the table by the window the night Payton went missing?" Cal asked him, indicating the table where the lookalike had sat.

"No. I wasn't here that night."

The report Jaslene had read said police talked to regulars who said they saw him. One said they saw him come in and another agreed with the waitress that he was sitting at the table until after ten.

"Riley sat next to me at the bar and left after two beers," Hewitt said.

The bartender turned from Cal to Hewitt, bewildered. "You sure?"

"Positive. He wasn't here very long. The guy who looked like Riley was here longer than Riley."

"How long?" Cal asked.

"I don't know. I left at nine and he was still here."

Jaslene turned at the same time as Cal and they shared a startled look.

Cal faced Hewitt again. "Tell us more about your conversation with Riley. Did he say where he was going after he left? Maybe explain why he left so early?"

Hewitt shook his head. "Just said he was leaving. I thought it was weird but didn't think anything of it. Then that girl went missing. Everybody talked about it here."

"Hewitt here is a regular but he doesn't come in regular, if you know what I'm saying," the bartender said.

"I work the night shift a lot. Don't come in when I work those odd hours." Hewitt's mouth turned down.

If he could come into this bar regularly as the bartender put it, he probably would. Jaslene wondered if something had transpired in his past to make him turn to alcohol. "What did you and Riley talk about?" Cal asked.

"Work. The weather. And he said his girlfriend broke up with him. He was pretty torn up about it, but he never told me her name."

"Tell me exactly what he said."

Jaslene all but held her breath and clenched her fists in anticipation.

"I asked if he was seeing anyone. We talked other times we sat together there, so I knew he wasn't married. I wasn't married, either." He held up his ringless hand. "Still not." He lowered his hand to the bar. "He said he was with her until she broke up with him. He didn't understand because he thought everything was good between them. He thought she needed time and she'd come around. I told him when a woman ends a relationship she doesn't go back. He didn't like hearing that. He said she'd come back. I told him he might not want to hope too much for that and asked what he'd do if she never did. All he said was, *'She will.'*"

He sounded certifiably crazy. What normal man would insist his ex-girlfriend would magically change her mind and come back to him?

"He finished his beer and paid his tab and left. I thought he left because of what I said."

Or had he left to commence an evil plan to kidnap Payton?

* * *

Cal drove away from the bar with Jaslene in the passenger seat. She was as quiet as him. He kept going over possibilities of Riley being involved in Payton's disappearance.

Riley's neighbors had said they saw him arrive home after ten, which corroborated the waitress's statement. Payton was seen leaving work at seven. Bank records showed she stopped at the market and paid for groceries at seven forty-five. Her neighbor witnessed her arriving home shortly after eight. Then her car was found the next day at a nearby park, abandoned. Had she driven there that night?

Had Riley waited for her in her house, done something to her and taken her to a park?

None of the neighbors reported noticing any strange vehicles and no one had seen her drive away from her house. Cal had found only two people who had been at the park after seven and neither had observed a car matching the description of Payton's. If she had been the one driving, she had gone to the park sometime after 8:00 p.m., which Cal had always found peculiar since the park was within walking distance of her house. If Riley had anything to do with her being there, then she would have had to arrive at the park before ten. There were no security cameras near the park.

Riley would have had plenty of time to commit a crime. He would have been able to be at Payton's house before she arrived home. Her phone records didn't show any calls to or from Riley that night, so Cal was sure Riley would have gone to her home and likely surprised her. There was no sign of a struggle at her house, and no sign a murder had been carried out there. Riley could have knocked her unconscious or threatened her at gunpoint and taken her to the park.

If Riley had driven his car to the park, it would have been after everyone had left.

If he could place him either at Payton's house or at the park, then he could give the police enough to take him in for questioning.

"It's getting late."

He turned to glance over at Jaslene and then realized he had passed the road to her house. Automatically he'd driven toward his.

"Are you hungry? Why don't you come over for dinner?" He didn't know why he'd asked. The words just tumbled out. "I'll have something delivered or we can pick something up. What sounds good?"

She didn't answer for a few seconds and another glance confirmed she was fumbling over how to respond. "Um…sure. I know a place on the way. It's a great deli. I don't want anything heavy."

He could do a sandwich and he liked not having to cook. He also liked the idea of spending some downtime with her. "Just tell me where."

Getting out of Cal's SUV, Jaslene had to take a moment to admire his house. Nothing could have surprised her more. The two-story Victorian home had white trim, shocking for a man who seemed to have sworn off family. The snow had melted except for the shady spots, revealing immaculately trimmed flower beds curving around the front of the house. The covered porch had outdoor furniture.

"Nice," she said as she walked with him to the white, arching front door.

"People who lived here previously fixed it up. I didn't have to do anything."

But something must have made him buy it. He might have tried to convince himself he'd never give love another chance, or set some stiff boundaries that would be near impossible to breach, but somewhere inside him hid a man who still yearned for what he'd thought he had with his wife.

Cal put his hand on her back, guiding her so she walked ahead of him. He'd unzipped his puffer jacket and she saw the dark gray Henley he wore. The textured shirt fit the hard slope of his chest well. Noticing he craned his neck to look behind them and at the street, she followed the direction of his gaze.

A car pulled out from the side of the street, driving slow toward them. The driver's window rolled down.

As soon as Jaslene saw that the driver wore a black balaclava and began to lift something in his right hand, she felt Cal shove her to the ground. She landed hard on her stomach just as gunfire erupted. Bark from the tree in Cal's front yard broke apart and flew to the dead grass.

Cal got up to kneel, returned fire and then took cover behind the tree. The gunman fired again.

Terrified, Jaslene covered her head with her arms, hearing bullets hit the ground nearby. Cal's gun fired in rapid succession as the car drove by and the shooter's gunfire paused momentarily.

Jaslene stayed low and crawled behind Cal and the tree, staying low but sitting on her hip and frantically peering around Cal and the tree to determine if the shooter had gone.

The gunman returned fire yet again. She made herself as small as possible behind the tree. Bullets kicked up dirt and grass as they hit the ground where she had just been crouching.

She heard the car speed up, tires squealing as it took a turn.

Cal fired a few more times and then bent to her. "Are you all right?" He checked her body and legs and felt her head, his eyes ablaze with what looked like adrenaline-fueled worry.

"Yes." She breathed heavily, trying to calm down.

"Go inside." He helped her up. "Lock the door." He removed a key from his key chain and handed it to her.

"What are you going to do?"

"Go inside." He ran to his SUV and got in and had the engine started and gear in Reverse before she even took a step.

Was he going to be all right?

She watched him peel out of the driveway and spin into a turn at the next street. The entire attack seemed to move in slow motion. What had taken seconds felt as though it had taken endless terrifying minutes.

Lights came on in the neighboring houses as some of Cal's neighbors began to emerge. Jaslene hurried to the door and inserted the key. She felt ill from fear. Her pulse still throbbed through her veins and her mouth was drier than a pretzel. Once inside, she locked the door behind her and let her forehead fall forward, breathing to finish calming her nervous system.

Jaslene heard sirens a few minutes later. She finally caught her breath and slowed her heart rate; the neighbors must have called the cops. Going to the front window, she looked through the glass, trying to see where Cal had gone. No sign of him yet.

One of the policemen spoke with a woman across the street, who must have been the one to call 911. When she pointed to Jaslene's house, several police walked over.

Feeling safe enough, she went back outside.

"Are you all right, ma'am?" the tallest of them asked.

"Yes. Someone in a mask drove by and shot at us. We just got out of the SUV and he started firing." She pointed to the tree. "That tree probably saved our lives."

"Our? Who else was here?"

"Cal Chelsey." She spotted his SUV coming around the corner. "There he is." She heard the great relief in her tone and felt it everywhere in her body.

The policemen turned and waited for Cal to pull into the driveway and park. He got out and hurried to Jaslene. He took her into his arms.

"Jaslene." He held her close. "I was so afraid you'd be hit."

His embrace was firm and full of emotion, as was his tone. His concern seemed out of character for him, a man who guarded so fiercely against love.

"I'm fine," she said with her mouth close to his ear.

He moved back but kept his arm around her as he turned to the police, another intimate gesture that indicated he acted in agreement with his heart, at least for now.

"Detective Chelsey," the policeman said. "Something must have changed in this case for someone to start shooting at you."

"Apparently so."

All they had done was talk to Dr. Benjamin and dig into Riley's alibi.

Riley's alibi.

Had he discovered what they had learned? He could be trying to stop them.

Cal explained what happened, including that there had been no plates on the car and he hadn't been able to find the driver in his chase. Cal hadn't seen where the other man had gone after he raced away. The police bade farewell and Jaslene turned to go back into Cal's house, seeing the neighbors had gathered in front yards to watch.

All the excitement had worn on her. She felt tired but in need of some pampering. She wanted to go home and take a bath but didn't think being alone was such a smart idea. She could be with Rapunzel.

Without adrenaline arresting her senses, Jaslene noticed the interior of Cal's home. His place looked homier than hers, yet another indicator that he had set up a haven for a family.

She removed her jacket and boots.

"This is the only furnished room other than my bedroom and another room upstairs," he said, as they walked into the living room. "I found it before my divorce and decided to buy it anyway since she took the house we were in."

She didn't miss how he said "took."

"A work in progress. It's quite lovely." And a shame to let such a wonder go empty. A house like this could turn her into an interior decorator.

"Thanks."

She faced him and found him watching her. Their eyes met and she couldn't look away. He seemed to be about to say something difficult.

"I don't think you should be alone," he said.

She didn't, either. "What about Rapunzel?"

"We can stay at your place."

She looked around again at his tasteful residence, feeling closer to the man who lived here. "I think I'd rather stay here." Stopping, she turned to him. "I know you are not a dog person but you might be now that you work for DAI. They might be more family oriented." She tested him by saying that.

He smiled. "If my coworker Roman is any indication, then yes, they are very family oriented."

He talked easily about others but what about himself?

"Why Roman?" she asked.

"He helped catch the man who killed his fiancée's sister. And family means the world to him."

Jaslene found that tantalizing. The single DAI detectives were desirable, indeed. When she began entertaining the possibilities of the same happening between her and Cal, she had to mentally block the fantasy. He was too distrusting. And she didn't feel good about risking her heart on him.

"Let's go get the critter and anything else you need." He went to the front window and checked outside. "I have a daybed in one of the other bedrooms. I'll make it up and sleep in there."

That was awfully kind of him, but Jaslene's dreams extended to testing him further: by sleeping with him. What would he do if he became intimate with a woman who wasn't his ex-wife? Temptation flared within her as she grew eager to find out.

After packing up clothes and toiletries for herself and also everything Rapunzel needed, Jaslene held the puppy in her arms all the way back to Cal's place. There had been no calls about her yet. She'd noticed him eyeing the dog as she packed three suitcases and a smaller bag. The back of his SUV was full of that and puppy necessities. She'd quipped, "Who knows how long I'll be with you."

"And here I thought you were more of a tomboy than a girlie-girl."

She had packed some clothes that qualified as sexy, telling herself she wasn't doing it for Cal. She didn't have much but what she did was only the best.

Now she entered his house again, this time carrying Rapunzel. The sun had long ago set and she was tired, but the day had been so eventful she didn't think she'd be able to sleep for a while. She struggled to pry off her boots and Cal helped her, having already removed his jacket and boots. In her stockinged feet, she let Cal help her remove her jacket without disturbing the puppy.

Adjusting the tiny fur ball in her arms, she followed Cal into the great room. "Do you have any wine?" They'd eaten sandwiches at her house earlier. "I could sip on a glass."

"Yeah." He went into his kitchen where she noticed a built-in wine bar and a refrigerator.

"I'll go get comfortable." She didn't allow any deep thoughts over what she was doing, only justified her actions as pure curiosity. Exactly how bitter was he when it came to women? If they made love, how would that change him, or would it? She needed to find out. "Are you sure you want me in your bedroom? I could sleep on the daybed."

"What kind of host would I be if I allowed my guest to sleep on a daybed?"

Smiling and not arguing, she looked down at a sleeping Rapunzel, hearing her tiny grunts, little protests over the movement disturbing her slumber.

Climbing the stairs, she went into Cal's room, where he'd taken her luggage, and gently lay the dog onto the bed, on the opposite side she planned to sleep. Rapunzel grunted again and opened her sweet eyes briefly, seeing her and then falling back to sleep.

She looked around the room at the crown molding, French doors leading to a balcony and sheer white curtains. That's where frilly ended.

She quietly changed into a silky pajama set, nothing too sexy…yet, but he might catch a few revealing glimpses of skin—enough to test him. She wasn't sure why she had decided to do that, only that she did want to know how he'd react.

Hearing him in the room across the hall, she went there and saw him making up the daybed. This room was painted a soothing and earthy yellow with more pretty white trim and crown molding. He finished the bed, making no fuss over tossing the pillows on the comforter. Straightening, he faced her and didn't move. Only his eyes lowered and slowly came back up, noticing her pajamas with distinct interest. She felt a surge of triumph, and maybe some relief to have the answer she had sought.

Wordlessly he approached. Jaslene stepped out into the hall and led the way to the living room, where she saw he'd turned on the fireplace and put two glasses of red wine on the coffee table.

Romantic? Or relaxing?

She sat on one of the sofas and reached for one of the wineglasses. Leaning back, she didn't see Cal. Sipping her wine, she looked over her shoulder and saw him peering out the front window. Realizing he checked for anyone suspicious, she felt a shiver raise bumps on her arms. He must have already checked the backyard from the window in the bedroom with the daybed.

Apparently satisfied no one lurked in the night, he walked to her. Before sitting, he removed his pistol from the holster at his waist and set it on the coffee table. She eyed it as he lifted his wineglass and leaned back.

"We're safe here," he said, taking a sip and putting his glass down on an end table.

The gun disturbed her because of how it reminded her that she'd almost been shot today. Cal, too. An image of Riley aiming his forefinger at them and pretending to pull the trigger kept going through her mind.

Cal stretched his arm around her, cupping her shoulder and tugging her closer.

She closed the few inches that separated them and gratefully accepted his offer of comfort. She also hadn't missed how his shirt molded to his muscular chest or how the black jeans mounded at his crotch.

"I won't let anything happen to you," he said.

He took her anxiety away just like that. After another sip of wine, she rested her head on his shoulder, believing him. He made her feel safe, and right now, tonight, safe not only physically, but emotionally.

He took her glass and set it next to his.

Jaslene closed her eyes, basking in the warm, safe feeling that washed over her. "When's the last time you were this close to a woman?"

The question had popped into her head and she'd blurted it out before she had time to think it over.

"Like this? A long time."

Lifting her head, she looked at his face. "But you've been close to a woman more recently?"

"Yes, but never anything serious."

Never, meaning he'd been close to more than one woman since his wife betrayed him. He'd had sexual relationships but nothing more. Cal might be bitter about love, but he didn't strike her as the type to dupe women into sex, only to dump them afterward.

"Well, savor it while you can," she said.

He chuckled. "I am."

She watched the flames Cal had lit in the fireplace for a while, wishing she knew if he'd ever be able to let go of his failed marriage and wondering why that was so important to her. She had not felt ready to be with another man since her husband died. Was she now ready? She thought she was, if for no other reason than to satisfy curiosity. She could sleep with him and not worry about him getting attached. Her only concern was if she fell for him and it hurt too much to walk away.

"Can I ask you a personal question?" she asked.

"We're already getting personal, sitting like this."

She smiled because that was true. "You're a good-looking man with a respectable job. You're also nice." She looked at him. "I don't understand how any woman would want to cheat on you."

"Thanks for the compliments, but I wasn't home at night a lot. She said she got lonely."

There had to be more to it than that. Why give up such a great catch? "Who was the man she slept with?"

"I didn't know him."

"That's not what I meant. Was he rich or something?"

"My ex-wife said she met him at a conference. She was a manager for a restaurant chain and they had some kind of team-building event at a hotel. He worked for his dad, who owned the hotel chain. He wasn't at the conference, but he was there to meet with the hotel manager."

"So he was loaded."

"My ex wasn't after money. If she was, she would have never married me."

"I wouldn't be so sure about that."

He picked up her glass of wine and handed it to her, then reached for his.

"She might not be worth all the emotion she left you with," Jaslene said, and sipped her wine.

"She would have left me regardless of what kind of man she found."

He sounded sure, and he wasn't an unintelligent man. He must have known his wife. Cal must have struggled so much over her betrayal. He couldn't be home for his wife when she needed him and she might have felt she needed to be taken care of.

Jaslene didn't think Cal blamed women for lack of integrity. She thought he felt slighted over not being able to be around when his woman needed him. He also didn't believe a woman existed who could tolerate that kind of schedule. As a private investigator, he would still work irregular and long hours.

"I dated a doctor once, a surgeon. I was in my early twenties and he was ten years older than me. We saw each other for almost a year. He was constantly called in or had to work nights and weekends. His schedule never bothered me."

"You were young." He drank some wine and set down his glass.

"True. I was in college. When he worked, I studied or spent time with my friends. I enjoyed my time alone. I still do."

She rested her head on his shoulder again. When she looked up at him again, he was staring into the fire with somber eyes.

He looked down at her and met her eyes for several seconds, then took in the rest of her face. "What ended the relationship?"

"He didn't seem that into me and I realized I wasn't that into him, either. He never wanted to be outside." She'd studied geology; of course she liked being outdoors. "I broke up with him. Funny, I thought since my dad was a doctor that this guy might be The One."

Cal grunted. "They say you can't chose the one you fall in love with." He sipped some more wine before asking, "How long after that did you meet your husband?"

"Not long, the next year. I met him in a calculus class and discovered his major was geology like mine, only he was a year ahead of me, which is why he wasn't in any of my core classes. He'd already taken them."

"He liked being outside."

She smiled. "Yes. We hiked and camped a lot and went on vacations to national parks."

"I like to camp." He put down his glass again. "I like barbecues, too." He grinned and made her laugh lightly.

That was outside. She couldn't knock him for that, but it wasn't hiking and going to parks. Maybe he thought he didn't have the time. He wouldn't work 24/7, 365 days a year. The important thing was he liked what she liked. They could find time to do them.

Being in a relationship, especially a marriage, meant both had to be flexible.

Without warning, he lowered his head and kissed her. She didn't think he planned it any more than she'd expected it. But the instant heat created tingles of pleasure all the way through her.

Something wet dribbled down on her pj's. Some must have dripped on him as well, since he jerked back the same time she did. She'd spilled her wine on them both. She looked up at him and laughed, and he joined her.

"It's time for bed anyway," he said.

Yes, bed…with him. Jaslene set down her glass and stood, the more practical side of her warning against the desire that moved her. But she had already made up her mind about this. She wasn't backing out now.

She turned and started for the stairs. Cal followed and she felt as much as heard his feet climbing each step behind her. She had ample time to change her mind and not invite him into her bed. Walking down the hall, she stopped at the doorway to his room. He stopped before her and she saw his sexy blue eyes ask where she'd have him sleep tonight.

Stepping aside, she let him pass her. She didn't know him well enough to fall for him. Not this soon. And she attributed her insatiable hunger for him to her long abstinence. In this modern world, she could satisfy her need and not feel obligated to offer commitment. She didn't think Cal would. Empowered with that justification, she unbuttoned her pajama top, going about the act slowly and seeing Cal's rapt sexual interest. More than that. She also saw intimate connection. His desire ran deeper than sex.

Encouraged by his look and what it conveyed, she let the top fall to the floor and stood still for his enjoyment. At last he pulled off his Henley. She stopped breathing for a second or two. His smooth skin rippled below the platform of his chest. The man stayed in great shape.

She pushed off her pajama pants and stood only in her underwear.

Cal continued to admire her as he unfastened his jeans and removed them along with his underwear. To be with a man, one not her husband, felt exciting and a little scary. The excitement kept her staring. No guilt or any other second thoughts plagued her and she realized why. This felt right. Just the ingredient she needed.

She hooked the hem of her underwear and worked them down, the rightness opening her soul and sharing this special time with him. She stood naked for him, not at all inhibited.

He took her in with ravenous eyes. Deliciously agonizing moments passed.

Just when she began to feel like too much of an exhibitionist, he stepped toward her. Her entire body heated with anticipation. When he stood close enough, he lifted his hands and touched her breasts, running his thumbs over her nipples and sending electric sensation spreading.

She took the time to glide her hands over his hard and smooth chest, something she'd been dying to do for some time now. She ran them down his rippling abdomen, too, then back up and on to his muscular shoulders.

Tipping her head back, she pressed her body against his as he lowered his mouth to hers. The riot of sensation intensified almost unbearably. She melded with him in unquenchable kisses. At last he moved her to the bed.

Cal pulled the sheet and comforter back and she lay on the bottom sheet. He followed on top of her and she opened her legs to receive him.

He kissed her mouth quickly several times and asked breathlessly, "What about protection?"

Why did he have to wait until now to ask that? "Do you have anything?"

"No."

She met his impassioned eyes and urgency to have him inside her made her do a quick calculation. "We should be okay."

"Are you sure?" He kissed her some more.

"Yes." She couldn't wait any longer. "Please don't stop. I'm so ready for you."

"Are you?"

She tipped her head up to kiss him and ran her tongue along his lips. "Why don't you find out for yourself?"

With a gruff sound, he began probing and sank into her, filling her and sending her into an out-of-mind experience. She gripped his hair as he thrust and then his buttocks, grinding herself against him until she burst.

He collapsed onto her and they caught their breaths together. Finally he lifted his head and looked at her.

"Are you sure that was safe?" he asked.

Jaslene could answer that in more than one way. And she was afraid the answer to both might be no.

Chapter 7

What happened with Jaslene left Cal in a near panic the next morning. The confusion of what felt like a life-altering experience put everything in disarray. His usual order of things were no more. He felt jittery and in need of escaping his own mind, or at least Jaslene. After waking early he'd left Jaslene in bed with Rapunzel snuggling close. He fought how much he liked the sight, and coffee with the news wasn't helping. He put down his cup on the kitchen counter.

Looking through the window above the sink, he watched it snow, medium flakes floating in breeze-less air. The most upsetting part about last night zeroed in on how different the sex had been from his ex. The possibility that he could have something real with Jaslene stared him in the face. What would he do now? He did not want a relationship, not another one like his marriage. He could fall hard for Jaslene. That could not happen.

What did she expect? She'd invited him into bed with her, but he didn't have to accept. Maybe he should have thought a little harder on the consequences.

Hearing her come into the kitchen, he turned. She'd taken a shower and dressed. Rapunzel pawed at her heels when she stopped. She didn't falter long, just looked at him and then headed for the back door.

"Come on, Rapunzel. Let's go potty." Opening the door, she let the puppy go outside.

He moved so he could see through the patio door. Rapunzel nearly fell headfirst as she navigated the step onto the patio. Then she stopped and sniffed the air, snorting as a flake hit her nose. She went about her business and then hurried in.

"At least I know she's trained," Jaslene said.

He could continue on with mundane chatter but they needed to talk. "Coffee?"

"Sure." Sitting down as Rapunzel found her food and water bowls, Jaslene watched him.

He poured her a cup. "Cream?"

"Yes."

By her definitive tone he guessed she liked a lot of cream and tried to give her enough to satisfy without ruining the taste of the coffee. Walking over to her, he set the cup down and then sat next to her around the corner of the high wood table.

"You look worried," she said with her hands around the cup.

He'd been that transparent? Grateful she'd broached the subject first, he said. "I want to talk about last night."

"No need. I knew what I was getting into."

Of all he'd anticipated having to deal with from her, this wasn't it. "What did you get into?"

She shrugged slightly and drank some coffee, all very nonchalant. "Just satisfying a curiosity. I don't want to have a boyfriend right now."

Was that what she preferred him to believe? He didn't think she felt much different than him—knew that they had explosive chemistry together.

"I'm not ready for that."

As she looked straight ahead, he realized her loss of her husband might have made her say that.

"It's been a while since your husband died," he said.

"Yes, and I'm over what happened...for the most part. I'm just not ready for a new relationship yet. I'm not sure when I will be."

"I can understand that." Should he be relieved? Funny, how he felt a little sting of rejection. "What part aren't you over yet?"

She looked at him. "Are you sure you want to hear that story?"

By that she must mean her "affair."

"Yes." Would she tell him the unvarnished truth? He almost didn't want to hear her tell him. If she'd had an affair, he could not be with her intimately. He had to stay true to himself in that regard.

Putting the cup on the table, she folded her hands and seemed to gather her thoughts. Cal wondered if she plotted how to tell him, give him the best story so he wouldn't think badly of her.

"I married Ryan when I was twenty-five. He died eight years later. We had a good relationship. I'd say it was more friendly than passionate, but we loved each other. Losing him was hard, but something that happened about two months before that made it even harder."

Her matter-of-fact way of stating that surprised him. He thought she'd ease into it with perhaps some exaggeration on her side of things. She told him the truth.

"I worked at another environmental firm at the time and frequently went on assignments with a coworker. His name was Ansel. He was German and spoke with an accent. He always had interesting stories to tell of his childhood and we spent a lot of time together working and got to know each other quite well. He knew I was married, but there was an attraction between us. I had no intention of acting on it. In fact, I felt guilty for having those feelings." She turned her head and looked down at her coffee cup. "Even then."

Cal could sense her deep regret and that she still felt guilty. He gave her credit for admitting that and better understood why she had been so reluctant to talk about it.

"I grew uncomfortable working with him. On one assignment we had to stay a few nights to collect data from the field. We had dinner that last night and he walked me to my room. He'd been very respectful of me and we had a nice time. Good food. Great conversation. And that spark." She moved her hands apart and fisted one on the table. "He ended up kissing me."

She looked at Cal and all the torment that kiss must have caused came through her eyes and struck him.

"He was immediately apologetic, but the damage was done. He went to his room and I went to mine. The next day, he left for the airport without me. He felt terrible…or maybe not terrible as much as angry with himself because he knew I wouldn't divorce Ryan to be with him. Back home, it was awkward at work, so I found another job and never saw him again."

Cal watched her remember that time. He could tell she'd had feelings for Ansel, maybe even still did, but she also had not forgiven herself.

Rapunzel finished at her food bowl and walked over to the rug before the patio doors. Curling up, she closed her eyes.

"I considered telling Ryan," she went on. "It bothered me so much. But really, what did I do? I had feelings for another man who kissed me. I didn't really do anything wrong other than stay at that job too long. I should have left long before I did."

"Did you kiss him back?" Cal asked, knowing it would be a difficult question for her to answer.

She averted her face and moisture gathered in her eyes. After several seconds and a quivering breath, she nodded. "It didn't last long, but yes."

He could tell that tore her apart more than anything. The revelation took Cal aback. He had not expected such a story. By all accounts she had tried to do right. She abstained from an affair and found a new job after Ansel had kissed her. She hadn't slept with him.

Wiping under her eyes, she said, "After Ryan died,

months turned into a year and the moments when I thought of Ansel lessened. They didn't go away, though. I couldn't stop thinking about how different it felt to kiss him than my husband. I think that is why I could never be honest and tell Ryan what happened, because if I did I'd have to also tell him I had more passion for another man than I'd ever felt with him."

She inhaled a deep breath and then let it go slowly, looking straight ahead, clearly heavy with thoughts of a man who wasn't her husband.

"Did he suspect anything?" Cal asked.

"Sometimes he'd ask if I was all right," she said, turning to him, "if he caught me in one of those moments when I thought of Ansel. I would always tell him yes. Things went on as they always had. We still enjoyed each other's company. We just never had that…spark."

"And then he died."

"He died so suddenly."

And terribly. Shot by a road rager.

"At first I had difficulty accepting the reality. I went through the funeral on autopilot. But then the weeks went by and the loss of him settled in. I missed him, but I didn't miss him the way a woman should if her husband dies—at least that's what I thought. I couldn't stand it when I thought of Ansel in those times. I should have been paying my respects to my husband. Instead I…"

She didn't finish. She didn't have to. Instead she had fantasies about another man.

"Men have asked me out on dates since his death

but I've always refused. I would feel too much like I betrayed him, and I had already betrayed him."

She still punished herself for having real feelings for another man after resisting him. Even Cal couldn't condemn her. Her situation was much different from his ex-wife's, who hadn't cared in the least about his feelings. Jaslene cared too much about her late husband's.

He sat with the first woman in a long time that he considered genuinely honest. That sort of disturbed him. If he trusted her, then what? They might get closer and he'd trust her more. Closer still and he could fall in love. Ask her to marry him. Then what? Time would pass and another man might come along. Maybe by then she wouldn't care anymore, just like his ex. The tumble in his gut was the result of apprehension. He didn't think he was ready.

"It's not your fault." He had to tell her that because it was true. "You didn't choose to fall for another man and you walked away. You didn't let your feelings lead you into an affair. You have nothing to feel guilty about, Jaslene."

She met his eyes for a few seconds. "Coming from you that means a lot." She smiled through what looked like a struggle to fend off tears.

He grinned. "It should." He was among the most distrustful men out there, he knew.

"Unfortunately, my heart isn't ready to believe that. Sleeping with you last night…" She looked away briefly. "It felt a lot like how I was with Ansel and that makes me uncomfortable. I need to keep this casual. Are you good with that?"

Another pang of rejection stung him, catching him unprepared. He hadn't expected her to say that. "Sure. I think you know I am."

She smiled, clearly relieved. "Yes, Mr. All-Women-Are-Cheaters."

Except you, he almost said.

Still smiling, she looked around his kitchen. "Which is strange. Why buy a house like this if you're going to be a bachelor the rest of your life?"

The rest of his life was a long time. "What's strange about my house?"

"It's…homey. Like a family belongs here."

"It's barely furnished."

"No, but it has everything else. I could help you with the furniture. I could get ideas from Tatum. It'd be fun to go shopping and fill this place up. It's such a gem. You shouldn't waste it. The previous owners took really good care of it."

"You really want to help me decorate?"

"Yes. I did the same with Ryan."

She must have gotten rid of a lot, then. Her house looked like a bachelorette pad.

"Why did you buy such a big house?" she asked. "You have four bedrooms and an office."

"I liked the house."

"Well." She put out her hands. "There you go. Then you should furnish it."

The sound of a cell phone ringing stopped him from responding. It was her phone. She stood and went into the living room. He listened to her answer and then her tone lowered as she gave directions to his house.

When she came back into the kitchen, she looked sad and had folded her arms. "Someone called about Rapunzel."

She'd have a hard time giving up the puppy.

And he would have a hard time giving up Jaslene, but he had to distance himself from her. She had the right idea: keep it casual.

Sitting on the sofa with Rapunzel on her lap, Jaslene was glad Cal had not caught on to how much their night together had altered her world. The spark between her and Cal was even stronger than the way Ansel had made her feel. That unsettled her no small amount. She'd known the first time she was with a man other than Ryan that it would be difficult, but she had to move on. She deserved pleasure but hadn't foreseen that she'd find it over and above anything else she'd ever experienced.

Would Cal's outlook on her change now that he knew she didn't have an affair? The idea of having a passionate relationship—even a marriage—with a man, to not have near-infidelity hanging over her head, tantalized her. Could she get involved and not feel terrible about Ryan? He'd died not knowing about Ansel. He'd died in a mediocre marriage. That wasn't fair. She still felt she owed him, but how did one make amends to a dead man?

She stroked Rapunzel's sleeping head. She didn't want to give her up. This kind of attachment felt safe, filled a void. The feeling of impending loss struck a sore spot in her heart.

The doorbell rang and her heart sank.

Cal went to answer and soon after an elderly man appeared, wearing a hat and a light gray vest with matching slacks. Quite the dapper gentleman, which only made her feel worse. Rapunzel appeared to belong to a good owner.

She stood and moved around the sofa.

"You must be Jaslene," the man said. "I'm Hank."

"Yes."

"And there's my little Spunky."

What an awful name.

"She is yours?" Jaslene asked. "Are you sure?"

"Yes, quite sure. My granddaughter got her for me as a birthday present. She surprised me."

Hank didn't move to take the dog but rather, eyed her with a certain amount of dread. "You've taken to her, it seems."

Jaslene smiled sadly. "I think I fell in love with her the moment I saw her in the rain."

"She ran off when I took the trash out. I didn't see where she went. Thank you for rescuing her."

Didn't he search for her? "I wouldn't have it any other way." She began to feel as though she should not give the dog back to him.

"I never thought I'd have another dog in my lifetime," Hank said. "My wife died a few years back and my family thought I was lonely."

"You sound as though you would rather not have a dog," Cal said.

"My granddaughter is upset that the puppy ran away. She might be hurt if I don't take her home. She knows I found her."

"You could leave her with me," Jaslene said. "She will have a good home. Could you explain that to your granddaughter?" She dared not let her burgeoning hope soar.

Hank looked at the puppy, still not taking her. "I'm too old and set in my ways to care for a dog. Dogs need food and water…and exercise. They need companionship."

Jaslene smiled. "Well, she has that with me, but it is up to you. She is your dog." She petted Rapunzel's head and bent her head to kiss her.

When she lifted her head, she saw Hank watching her, his light gray eyes now smiling. "No. You keep her. I'll find a way to make my granddaughter understand."

Jaslene couldn't hold back a giant smile. "Really?"

"Yes, really. I never wanted another dog. It wouldn't be fair to raise this one in a home like that. She'll obviously get more attention with you."

Rapunzel opened her eyes and looked up at her.

"I promise you, she will."

"My granddaughter will have to learn not to give people presents with beating hearts unless they're sure it's what they want. She didn't even ask me what kind of dog I liked, and especially if I even wanted a dog. I had words with her mother already. Why did she allow her child to get an animal as a present?" The elderly man chuckled with affection.

Jaslene smiled. "Your granddaughter must have the powers of persuasion."

"She has the power to sway my heart, that's for sure.

She's just like her mother that way. Always getting her way because one sweet look is all it ever takes."

She saw Cal's mouth curve up with that and wondered if the image of a loving family had caused it. This man clearly loved his daughter and granddaughter and likely would have raised the puppy despite his reluctance.

"I'll tell them Spunky is adjusted to another home and I didn't have the heart to take her away from her new owners."

"You may want to add a cautionary note not to get you another dog to replace the one you lost," Cal said.

"Very good advice. I'll be sure and do that." The elderly man turned and headed for the door. "I thank you for taking the dog in."

"Thank you for coming by," Jaslene said, going to the front entry. "And for letting me keep her."

Grinning broader now, Cal moved beside her and put his hand on her back. She looked up at him, warmed by his seemingly unconscious gesture.

When she looked toward the door, she saw that the man faced them and must have witnessed the exchange.

"I looked at my wife that way when we first met. We were together more than sixty years and I never had a second thought about the rightness." He nodded once. "You two are going to be happy together."

Cal's hand dropped from her back and he cleared his throat.

Jaslene tried to conceal the swelling warmth spreading from her heart outward, not because she found his awkwardness amusing but rather because of what it said about his reaction to such an observation, as though Cal fought the truth but it enchanted him. Cal must not have been aware of the way he had looked at her.

The elderly Hank left with another chuckle. The door closed and she stood there with Cal.

"He's a nice man," she said, scratching Rapunzel's head.

"Reasonable."

"What if he's right?" She faced him, feeling the urge to poke at his emotional barriers.

His head lowered in gentle debate. "He was here for fifteen minutes. How can anyone know anything about strangers in that amount of time?"

"Maybe he doesn't need to know us. All he said was he used to look at his wife that way."

"Did he have a mirror? How can he know how he looked at his wife?" He turned and walked back into the living room.

She followed. "His wife must have told him."

He passed through the living room and went into the kitchen, going to the refrigerator. Taking out a bottle of water and twisting the cap off, he met her eyes in consternation.

Though she could see he wouldn't respond, she wasn't ready to stop poking. She walked to him as he drank several gulps of water.

When he finished, she stepped close and went up on her toes and planted a soft kiss to his lips.

An instant flame burst into tingles of desire, proving their chemistry. When she saw something in his eyes begin to smolder, she knew he felt it, too.

"That's what he saw," she said.

"I thought you wanted to keep this casual." His voice sounded deep and gruff, as though passion had injected hot spice into his tone.

"I do." She turned.

"What's casual about contemplating the next sixty years together?"

"Nothing." She kept walking. "He just got me thinking, that's all." About spending the next sixty years with Cal...

Holy cats. Why had she allowed herself to poke at Cal? To get his reaction, yes, but really...why had she? Did she harbor some hidden desire to be with him permanently? She couldn't wrap her mind around that right now. But she did have what she secretly desired... She'd seen what the elderly man had seen: Cal looking at her with passion—and maybe something more—in his eyes.

Chapter 8

Nothing new developed in the case over the next three weeks. Jaslene and Rapunzel had temporarily moved in with Cal, which had not been easy. Jaslene had chosen to put distance between them, as much for herself as for him. They hadn't slept together again; he wasn't any better equipped to deal with the emotional fallout from their hot, steamy night any more than she was. Living together made close contact difficult to avoid. He had nearly kissed her twice but stopped himself. He wasn't sure exactly what she meant by keeping things casual between them but he was pretty sure if they had sex again it would be anything but casual.

Right now she folded laundry while he worked. He rarely went into his office, claiming he didn't want to leave her alone, even inside the house. She'd considered going back to work, but she wanted to be a part of the investigation. She'd taken some leave and she'd stick to that. She also had a sizable life insurance benefit from Ryan.

She and Cal had kept tabs on Riley's home, work and places he frequented but the man seemed to have disappeared just as Payton had. Neighbors had reported seeing him the day Cal had chased him, but no one had seen him leave his apartment. One neighbor said she heard a motorcycle engine but couldn't be sure if it was Riley's. Conducting surveillance put Jaslene and Cal in close proximity. Their conversations were few, but always she felt the impact of their explosive chemistry underlying their interactions.

They'd followed up with Dr. Benjamin's employees and acquaintances as well. No one else had anything negative to say about him, and if he'd had an affair, he had kept it a tightly locked secret. Nurses said he had impeccable bedside manner and patients respected him. He had a genuine care for humankind as a whole, strong ethics when it came to the law, respect for patients' rights and confidentiality, and supported ongoing advancement of knowledge and sharing information with patients. Had he threatened people not to say anything incriminating? Had he paid them off? If a doctor like him would go to any length to protect his reputation, why would he risk meeting Payton in public?

Jaslene and Cal had found no other concrete evidence that Dr. Benjamin had engaged in other questionable interactions with specific patients. Everybody slipped up, didn't they? Maybe he'd only been trying to be friendly.

She folded the last towel and brought it up to the main bathroom, hearing the phone ring on the way. Heading back downstairs, she now heard Cal in his office, ending what sounded like a personal call.

Seeing him come out of the room at the front of the house and off the living room, she stopped. His face was drawn with worry.

"My mother had a minor stroke," he said, sounding shocked.

She could imagine what he felt. He'd estranged himself from his family and now his mother's health had taken a turn.

"I have to go there."

"Of course. You should."

"You have to go with me."

Whoa. "What? To see your family? I don't think so. I'll go stay with mine while you're away. I won't be alone."

He shook his head. "You aren't getting out of my sight. I can't deal with that on top of my mother." *And the state of relations with my family*, Jaslene could almost hear him think.

"Do you have someone to watch Rapunzel?"

She didn't like the idea of leaving the puppy with anyone else. The poor dog had gone from one home to another.

"We won't be gone long."

"My sister is a dog person. I'll ask her." She went to him. "Is your mother going to be all right?"

"I think so. It was a minor stroke. My dad called

it a transient ischemic attack and said the doctors are worried that may lead to a full-blown stroke in a matter of months. She needs treatment."

He seemed unable to comprehend that something like this had happened to his mother. Jaslene put her hand on his muscular shoulder, wanting to comfort him somehow.

"Nobody is invincible," she said. "At least she didn't have a full-blown stroke *first*."

"My whole family is invincible. She's probably driving the doctors nuts with all her bossing around."

Jaslene smiled. "Good for her."

"She won't lie down for a medical condition. She may not accept she has one and go on as though nothing happened."

Cal dealt with so much death in his job, she could see how he'd be the more rational one in his family. The Chelseys might be aggressively ambitious, but Cal had his own brand of success.

Jaslene couldn't wait to meet his family. They sounded like an interesting group of people. And she'd bet Cal was closer to them than he let on. Maybe getting to know them would give her more insight into his bias about love.

The next day, Jaslene's sister agreed to watch Rapunzel, who'd warmed right up to her the moment Jaslene had dropped her off. Apparently, she had a social dog. That hadn't remedied her reluctance to be away from the runaway. Canines were pack animals. They needed to be a part of a family unit.

Jaslene realized how much she'd bonded with the

puppy and had to let go. Rapunzel was warm, safe and dry and she'd remain so until Jaslene returned. Cal would stay in touch with police in their search for Riley and she would feel safer several states away while they did.

They had arrived in Texas by plane and now drove toward Cal's family's ranch. She glanced over at Cal.

He stayed quiet all the way to Texas, though his mother had been released from the hospital when they drove. She'd asked questions but he'd been vague. The little he'd told her included the facts his parents had two homes, one in Irving and the ranch far outside the city of Dallas. She had gathered they had money. Growing up a doctor's child, she hadn't wanted for anything, but she had a feeling her parents were different from Cal's financially and emotionally. Her parents raised their kids in a small town and had always been there for them, supportive and happy.

Cal drove the rented dark blue Buick through a grand iron gate and up a long, paved drive.

"Wow. Impressive," she said. "How could you leave all of this?" He would have had it made.

"It's not important to me."

Helping people, victims and families of victims, was important. She felt even more of a connection to him. He didn't place much importance on the wealth of his parents, or money in general. To her, living a good life meant doing what made her happy and feel fulfilled and treating people the way she liked to be treated. Cal had devoted his life's work to avenging the dead. He was a true hero in her eyes.

As the tree-lined road cleared, a redbrick Tudor came into view, behind a stone circle drive fit for a mansion, and the shrub-bordered front entrance. She wouldn't call this house a mansion by size alone, but it might as well be.

"I feel terribly underdressed," she said.

"Don't let them make you feel that way."

Cal parked behind three other cars and then retrieved their luggage. He rang the bell, something Jaslene found peculiar.

A man who looked strikingly similar to Cal answered. Nearly as tall as Cal, he wore expensive-looking loafers and a smartwatch.

"Well, if it isn't my long-lost brother." He stuck out a hand. "How've you been, bro?"

His attempt to sound casual fell flat even to Jaslene, who knew nothing about this man.

"Corbin." Cal shook his hand briefly and then put his hand on Jaslene's back to let her in through the doorway first. "This is Jaslene Chabot."

"Chabot. Are you French?"

She almost scoffed but covered the reaction with a short breath. What an odd thing to say upon first meeting someone. "Maybe somewhere down the line. I'm American."

"Ah," he responded neutrally.

Did he really think she'd be from France or was he just fishing for something to say?

"How's Mom?"

"She's been asking about you." Corbin turned and led them through the paneled entry flanked by two curving stairs. Beyond the arch created by the grand staircase, a large living room spread to a wall of white-framed windows. Quite a vision upon first entry.

"When we told her you were coming, she brightened. Why haven't you come back before now anyway? Are we too good for you?" Corbin winked back at Cal but Jaslene sensed he wasn't completely kidding.

Cal didn't respond as they climbed to the second level and onto a wide, open landing where two sets of double doors opened to a huge library. Past the stairs, two hallways branched off in opposite directions.

Cal put his luggage at the top of the stairs and Jaslene did, too, then followed him to the left. At the end of the hall, double doors opened to an enormous master bedroom with a canopied king bed and entire seating area before a fireplace and wall-hung TV above.

A blonde woman smiled as they entered the room, her bright green eyes rimmed with dark liner and mascara, lips shiny red. In a black-and-white fitted dress, she wore high heels and diamond earrings and necklace. Jaslene could see her massive wedding ring from here.

On the bed an older woman with sharply bobbed, graying dark hair spoke in a low volume to a tall, lean man in a suit with brown hair showing gray as well.

The woman saw them and she drew in a breath. "Cal." She stuck out her arms. The man, who must be Cal's father, stepped back to give his son room.

Cal went to his mother and bent to hug her. "Hello, Mother."

Jaslene heard his tone and knew instantly that he

loved his mother. She could see the way his father watched and eyed Cal with reticence and a trace of irritation. Cal's escape from Texas still didn't sit well with him, apparently.

"How are you feeling?" Cal asked as he withdrew. "And don't give me your sass."

She swatted her hand through the air above the taupe comforter folded up to her stomach. "I'm fine. Everyone is fussing over me too much. The doctors gave me medicine." She looked up at Cal and gave a frustrated sigh. "I'll take it."

"You better." He turned at last to his father. "Dad."

"Son."

It was the stiffest greeting she'd ever witnessed among family members.

"Who's this you have with you?" his mother asked, peering around Cal's body to see Jaslene.

"This is Jaslene Chabot, everyone. I'm working a case with her."

"Hello," Jaslene said to Cal's mother.

"I'll bet you're working a lot more than that," Corbin said.

"Stop being such a showman, Corbin," said another woman, sitting on the couch. "You're not that spectacular."

Corbin scowled.

"This is my father, Newman, and my mother, Francesca." Cal ignored his brother's comment but added, "That's Corbin's wife, Ambrosia."

This was getting more interesting by the second.

Nodding to a woman on the couch with long, thick,

black hair in jeans and a red Western blouse, Cal added, "That cowgirl over there is my little sister, Skylar."

Jaslene smiled at her. "Nice to meet you." She couldn't express how nice it really was, to have this glimpse into more of Cal.

"Come sit with me," Skylar said. "I'll save you from Corbin and my dad."

Cal sat on the bed and started up a conversation with Francesca that Jaslene couldn't hear. Newman looked on as though he held back from joining in. Corbin and his wife went to the foot of the bed and left Jaslene alone with Skylar.

Jaslene sat on the sofa, seeing a cowboy hat on the cushion beside Skylar.

"Are you a detective like Cal?" Skylar asked.

"No. He's helping me find a friend of mine who's gone missing."

Skylar's friendly face scrunched up. "Oh, I'm so sorry."

"We'll find her. Cal isn't the giving-up kind."

"Only if you exclude his family in that assessment." Skylar looked away and toward the crowd around Francesca. They all seemed close to her, more of a family unit than Cal had described. His father did line up to what Cal had told her, and his brother, too, but not Francesca and Skylar.

"Did he tell you why he left Texas?" Jaslene asked.

"He married a woman who wanted to be closer to her family." Skylar faced her again. "Did he tell you about her?"

"Only that she destroyed his faith in women." She

smiled at the twinkle in Skylar's eyes. "He told me that he caught her with another man."

"Don't let that deter you. Cal is a lover at heart. I think that's why he used the dingbat as an excuse to stay away. He was too much of a romantic to keep up with Corbin and Dad."

"I don't think he cares about keeping up with anyone. Cal has set his own rules about how to live."

"Oh, trust me I know. I'm not saying he's weak. He just needs more out of life than Corbin." She glanced over. "Take Ambrosia, for example. Corbin only cares about being successful and having possessions that include a beautiful wife. She was a lingerie model. That's the only reason my brother married her. He likes everyone looking at him with envy. She might as well be a plaque on the wall."

Jaslene agreed, but some women found happiness in having a man who took care of them. Perhaps Ambrosia was content.

"My father is just plain ruthless in our oil business." She looked around the room. "How do you think we got all of this? Cal's right that our dad and brother are materialistic and greedy. I believe those are the words my brother would use."

"Yes, they are."

Skylar angled her head as she scrutinized Jaslene. "Wow. You two have talked a lot. It's more than a case between you, isn't it?"

Jaslene chose not to go there just yet. "Your mother doesn't seem like she was ever a trophy wife."

"Okay, I'll wait until we get to know each other

better." Skylar's easy acceptance of Jaslene's preference to keep some things private drew Jaslene to her even more. "She isn't a trophy wife. My father will never admit how much he adores her, either. He's sort of an ass when it comes to love. My mother knows it and plays him like a fiddle. He's putty in her hands."

Jaslene laughed softly, not wanting anyone else to catch on. "I think I just met my next good friend."

Sitting at the long, formal dining room table next to Jaslene later that night, Cal became increasingly uncomfortable with how chummy she and his little sister had become in such a short period of time. Eyeing Skylar, he placed a bowl of mashed potatoes in front of Jaslene. Sometimes his parents hired help to do the serving but not when it was just family.

As Jaslene scooped some potatoes onto her plate, Skylar, seated next to her, grinned slyly and then sipped some white wine.

He caught his father watching him again from his throne-like chair at the end of the table. Brooding, more like. Mother was asleep upstairs so it was just him, Jaslene and Skylar on this side of the table and his brother and his vacuous wife across from them.

"Why don't you tell us about yourself, Jaslene?" his dad said. "Is your family from Chesterville?"

Jaslene brightened as she always did when she had an opportunity to talk about her family. "Yes. All of us. I have two brothers and a sister. My parents took an early retirement."

"What did your father do?"

"He's a doctor. A surgeon."

Cal despised how his father's interest grew. A doctor was someone he could respect. Had Jaslene's father been someone lesser in his mind, like a mechanic or a carpenter, his reaction would have been considerably duller.

"My older brother, Darian, is an ear, nose and throat doctor. The youngest, Taber, is in college for engineering, and my older sister, Caley, is a…what would you call her…a jet-setter, I suppose. She married the son of a television executive."

"Ah. Impressive."

"I'm not sure if you'd call my sister impressive." Jaslene breathed a laugh as she scooped vegetables onto her plate. "I love her to death but she's a bit of a wanderer. So is her husband, with all his money, so I suppose they make a good pair."

Cal looked over at Corbin, who glanced at his wife as though showing her off. Corbin smirked.

"And what is your profession?" Newman asked. "Cal's last wife was a manager of a restaurant chain."

Cal turned to his callous father but kept his face expressionless, refusing to give him the satisfaction of a reaction.

"I'm a geologist. I took a leave from work to look for a friend of mine. Cal is helping me."

"She's a missing person," Skylar said.

"Cal left the Chesterville police force to take her case," Jaslene said. "He joined a private investigation firm called Dark Alley Investigations."

Cal remained a quiet observer, seeing his father's

unspoken disapproval climb higher. "That sounds like something out of a Hollywood movie."

"Actually, Kadin Tandy, the founder of DAI, is considering doing a television show about some of the cases he and his detectives have solved," Cal said.

"Tandy?" his father said. "Never heard of him."

"You wouldn't," Cal could not resist saying. "He isn't into oil and guns."

"It isn't oil I'm *into*, son. It's money."

"Pardon me. My mistake."

His father gave him a contemplative but condescending look and then turned back to Jaslene. "I never understood why Cal stayed in Chesterville after his divorce."

Jaslene finished a bite of food and swallowed, fingering her wineglass. "Well, if he's anything like me and my family, he likes the community."

"Pie festivals and church?"

"There are festivals." Jaslene nodded but met Newman's insulting eyes with a frigid expression that Cal had never seen before. "Have you ever been to a small-town festival, Mr. Chelsey?"

"Thank goodness, no. My tastes are more…big city, if you will."

"Well, then." Jaslene picked up her wine and sent Newman another frosty look. "In that case, I don't think you know enough to judge."

Skylar snorted as a laugh burst from her and Cal grinned, meeting Jaslene's eyes and hoping she saw the *bravo* in his. Now she'd understand why he'd left all those years ago.

But Jaslene wasn't finished, he discovered.

"Maybe you should plan a visit to your son some-time. He could show you around. I hear you've never been there, much less called to talk to him."

Newman's stony expression met hers for several tense seconds.

"I'm getting tired." *More like bored.* Ambrosia scooted her chair back. The company probably wasn't glitzy enough for her. "If you'll excuse me." Then to her husband, she said, "Darling."

"I'll join you. It's been a real treat seeing you again, Cal. You heading back tomorrow?"

"Maybe. I want to spend some more time with Mother."

"Until morning, then."

Cal noticed how his father averted his gaze at the mention of his mother. He was genuinely concerned for her. His love for Francesca was his only redeeming quality. The thought of losing her must be eating him up. For a second he almost felt sorry for him. But only a second.

Jaslene followed Cal's father as he led them to their rooms. Cal trailed behind, seeming a little melancholy. They were staying in his family home, but Skylar, she had discovered, had her own house somewhere on the ranch property. She'd quipped just before she'd left that she wouldn't be able to stand living with her parents. Corbin lived in Dallas, having no desire for ranching—the one difference between him and his father.

"The housekeeper brought your luggage to your

room," Newman said, stopping at a door at the end of a short hall off the living room. Jaslene looked behind her and to her sides. This was the only doorway.

"Uh…"

"Come on, Jaslene." He guided her into the room and faced the doorway. "Thanks, Dad." He shut the door.

She spun to face him. "Why did you do that?"

"I want you close, for one." He walked over to the bed. This was another master suite like his parents' room, only less formal and more welcoming. A blue-and-white comforter and a colorful painting brightened the room. The seating area wasn't as large, with only two blue chairs on a white rug before a fireplace.

"And for another?" she asked.

"I didn't feel like explaining anything to my dad."

"He thinks we're a couple and that isn't true."

"It's kind of true." He hefted the suitcases on the stands located in front of the windows.

Jaslene went there and opened hers, digging out a comfortable but practical nightgown. Cal removed his shirt and shoes, then went into the bathroom to wash his face.

With the evening's events running through her mind, she went to the other of the two sinks.

"Your sister is nice," she said.

He finished drying his face and looked at her in the mirror. "Yes."

"So is your mother."

"What are you trying to say, Jaslene?"

He sounded taxed from the hours spent with family

he wanted nothing to do with, and yet he'd flown back to Dallas at the drop of a hat as soon as he'd heard his mother had a ministroke.

"It's not your entire family that's annoying," she said. "Your brother and father have a…strange way of viewing the world, but your sister and mother are fine."

"Except for the fact that, in order to see them, I'd also have to see Newman and Corbin."

"I still think you should talk to your dad. Corbin would probably follow his lead if you patched things up. Your father's approval seems really important to him."

Cal suddenly removed his jeans, taking Jaslene by surprise. He stopped in the doorway where she stood.

"Don't worry. I'm too tired to do anything but fall asleep as soon as my head hits the pillow."

After watching him walk to the bed and admiring his butt, she took her time in the bathroom.

When she emerged, Cal lay on the bed, blankets up to his chest, but exposing his nipples. He had not fallen asleep when his head hit the pillow. His head wasn't even on the pillow. It was on his folded arm, bulging his muscles.

The TV played at a low volume. Jaslene went to the bed, nervous about sleeping with him. She climbed under the covers and lay looking up at the ceiling.

"I thought you were tired," she said.

"I thought so, too."

He must be thinking about his father, being back here.

Jaslene rolled onto her side, propping her head on

her hand, the covers under her other arm. "Your mother was glad to see you."

Smiling warmly, he turned his head. "Yeah."

Once he had told her that he didn't come back because he didn't want to see his dad. Jaslene thought he had a bad habit of avoiding his problems. She needed a gentle way of broaching that with him.

"It must be hard to deal with all the death in your line of work and then have to face things that don't turn out the way you would like in your personal life."

He rolled his head straight again. "Jaslene…"

He didn't sound terribly angry…yet. "All I'm saying is, you have enough to deal with in your job."

"You're saying more than that. Stop sugarcoating and say what you want to say."

"Are you sure? I don't want to overstep a boundary." She wanted to help him grow past his ex, whom she now knew was named Megan.

"Yes, go ahead."

He seemed genuinely all right with her talking about this. "Well," she put her hand on his torso and rubbed slowly. "Maybe you haven't gotten over Megan and haven't forgiven your father yet because you can't."

Cal looked from where her hand rubbed to her. "I don't follow."

"You don't want to do the work it will take to resolve the way you feel," she said.

"And how would I go about doing that?"

"You could start by talking to your father."

He looked up at the ceiling, brow going marginally

low. "That's probably going to be inevitable. I'll have to talk to him, whether I want to or not."

"Tell him how you feel, Cal." Jaslene stopped rubbing but left her hand there.

"I have. Many times. It doesn't work."

"Have you ever vanished for three years before?"

He sighed and met her gaze and she could see he had not.

"Maybe he'll listen this time. Give him a chance."

Cal didn't respond for a few seconds. "What about Megan? I don't want to talk to her."

Jaslene rested her head on his folded arm and began running her finger along his chest. "She's a different matter."

"I can't wait to hear your suggestion." He sounded sarcastic but not irritated.

"Her you just have to chalk up to a mistake, learn from it and put it behind you. Stop overprotecting your heart, Cal. Don't let her have that kind of hold over you."

"Huh. Easier said than done."

"You can still have what you wanted with someone else."

He turned his head and their faces were closer. "You?"

She hadn't meant to imply herself, but now that she had she would go with it. "The jury is still deliberating on that."

He chuckled and took hold of her hand, stopping the drawing on his chest. "It is."

Cal moved her hand down until he placed it over his

erection. All the while they'd talked he'd been lying there getting aroused.

As he kissed her, his response kept going through her mind. He would still hold back with her but as passion grew it ceased to matter.

Chapter 9

Cal woke up early the next morning and left Jaslene sleeping lest they ignite another inferno. He had surprised himself by being receptive to talking about his dad and Megan with Jaslene. Truth be told, he wanted to hear what Jaslene had to say. He wanted to know how to get past his personal demons. Talking to his dad, he could do. Letting Megan go would be harder. Not letting her go; he had let go of her the day he had discovered her betrayal. He had to let go of his bitterness. Jaslene was melting into his heart. Look at him; he was thinking of Megan by her name now. That had to be because of Jaslene. He and Jaslene were so good together. Therein lay the problem. Whenever he considered giving something serious a try, he got cold all over.

He saw his dad was alone at the kitchen island bar, sitting on a stool with a cup of coffee and his tablet, working no doubt.

Reluctantly, Cal went to the cabinet and found a cup, then poured fresh coffee that smelled like only the best money could buy.

"Phyllis made breakfast," his dad said with a brief glance his way. "It's on the table."

Phyllis was the housekeeper-slash-cook. Cal looked behind him and saw the spread, kept warm in catering pans. "Does she work through tonight's dinner, too?"

Now his father held his gaze. "No, we have a night staff to make it for us."

Cal took his cup and sat a chair over from his dad. Maybe he and Jaslene would go home today. He felt the tension between himself and his father, the difficulty he always had with him socially. They might as well be strangers.

"Your brother has always been envious of you."

Cal didn't expect his dad to say something like that.

"That's why he's always taking jabs at you," his dad said, sipping some coffee with his gaze still on the tablet.

"What about his wife? Am I supposed to be impressed?"

Newman grunted with a grin and glanced at Cal; for the first time in a long while, Cal felt any sliver of a connection with his father. "No. That's Corbin trying to feel like as much of a man as you are."

Cal could only gape at his father. "You think I'm a man?"

"Takes a pair of *huevos* to do what you do. And now you've joined that agency. I never got to tell you I was proud of what you've done with your life, Cal. The rangers. Your degree. Becoming a homicide detective."

Seeing the sincerity in his dad's eyes, Cal wondered if he'd finally reached an age where wisdom had finally kicked in. "Did Mother put you up to this?" He had to ask.

His dad grinned again. "No. And for the record, I still don't like your political orientation."

Because it didn't align with his.

"How's business?"

"The ranch is running great with Skylar managing everything."

Cal felt a further softening toward his father, but held back in case this was just a lapse in his ordinarily cutthroat operation. "I meant your business."

"Aw, now, Cal, you know this ranch is my first love."

Cal had to take a moment to digest that. He had never perceived his father to be a rancher first and top corporate executive second. "Actually, I didn't."

His father met his eyes as the realization his son hadn't known hit him. "You and I never had much chance to talk after your divorce and you decided to stay in that little southeastern town."

This was the most they had talked in years. "Why didn't you come home for a visit before this?"

"I called."

"On holidays. Hardly the time to have a father-son talk. And the phone... I guess I didn't know how to broach the subject. And I knew you were hurt over Megan. I wanted to give you time."

Cal could appreciate his dad giving him space, but wasn't three years a little much?

"I can't lie and say I don't enjoy working corporate," his dad said. "I do. But this ranch means everything to me. It's my legacy, what I'll leave to my children. The three of you and your mother are more important to me than anything, more than my success as an executive. As soon as I heard you were coming here, I decided I had to tell you that."

"Thanks, Dad."

His dad smiled slightly, warmly. "Will you come see us more, son? Your mother…"

"Yeah." Cal looked away. While a ministroke hadn't killed Francesca, she was at risk of a bigger one. Her life could end at any time. Cal wouldn't waste time. "I will."

His dad put his hand over Cal's and gave him a few pats. "I'll work on Corbin but I can't promise he won't continue to be annoying."

"I can handle Corbin."

His dad returned his attention to his tablet. "What about that girl you brought? How long have you been seeing her?"

"I'm not seeing her."

His dad turned to him. "Looks to me like you are. Was I mistaken in putting you in the same room?"

"No." Cal never got uncomfortable around family but with this new turn in his relationship with his dad, he felt that way now. "I need her close to protect her."

"But you're already close, aren't you?"

"I don't know her that well."

His dad studied him while he appeared to mull over that. "I see."

What did he mean? Cal continued to look at him.

"You aren't seeing her but you two have something going on. I get it."

His dad had never spoken this casually to him. "What's changed in you?"

His father's brows twitched. "Changed?"

"Yeah. You usually aren't this nice to me," Cal half joked.

His dad chuckled briefly before he sobered. "When your mom…" He rubbed his forehead.

"Where were you when it happened?"

He sighed. "Work." He turned to Cal. "Skylar called and said the ambulance was on the way. I had my corporate helicopter take me to the hospital. When I got there, Skylar told me Francesca called her and she couldn't understand what she was saying. She called 911 on her way to the house. The doctors said she had a stroke and tests were being done to determine how severe."

Cal could imagine how the waiting must have tortured him.

"I was baffled. How could she have had a stroke? Corbin arrived and finally we were allowed to go in the emergency room to see her. When she smiled and said she was fine, I never felt more relieved in my life."

"Test came back with a mini?"

"Yes." His dad rubbed his face this time, clearly agitated. "I don't know what I would do without her, Cal."

"She'll be around for a long time, Dad. She isn't the lying-down kind. She loves this ranch as much as you do. She's a hard worker and has been healthy, other than the stroke, hasn't she?"

His dad nodded. "Yeah, but I still am afraid."

This time Cal put his hand on his father's. "No matter what happens we'll all be here for you."

His father shook off his melancholy, his emotion something so rarely seen in such a man. "I'll be all right on my own, I just can't bear the thought of living without my Francesca."

Cal grinned at first and then couldn't stop a chuckle. "The iron man falls at the feet of a woman. I always knew you loved her but this is pretty pathetic, Dad."

His dad half smiled. "Don't tell anyone."

Hearing the front door open, Jaslene left her eavesdropping spot and went into the kitchen. She'd been about to enter when she heard Cal and his father talking and stopped short. She heard Cal ask why his father hadn't called and couldn't stop listening after that. Yawning to cover up the guilt over intruding on a private conversation, she went to the coffee machine, feeling Cal watch her.

She inwardly cheered for Cal bonding with his father—finally. She also wondered how Newman could tell there was something going on between her and Cal.

As she turned to take her coffee to the table behind Cal and Newman, Skylar entered, dressed in Wranglers, boots, a flannel shirt and cowgirl hat. Her presence zapped energy into the room.

"How's Mom?" she asked.

Seeing food had been put out on the table, she took a plate from a stack and scooped eggs and potatoes onto it along with some fruit.

"I almost had to tie her down to keep her from getting out of bed," Newman said. "Phyllis is up with her now, probably force-feeding her."

Skylar smiled and poured some coffee. "She'll be down shortly. Just let her be."

Newman looked up with what Jaslene imagined was an unappreciative glance. Then he finished his coffee and stood, bending to put the tablet in his leather laptop case.

"I've got to go into the office for a while. Will you be here for dinner?" he asked Cal.

Cal glanced at Jaslene and then said, "Yes."

His dad nodded once, back to his unapproachable self.

"Bye, Dad," Skylar called.

"Daughter." Newman left and Cal went to sit at the table, putting a plate of food together.

Skylar joined them, eyeing the two of them as she ate.

"Jaslene, would you like me to give you a tour of the ranch?" she asked.

She'd love that. "Yes. I really would." She turned to Cal. "Will you join us?"

"This is a girls-only tour," Skylar cut in.

Cal smiled and said, "I want to spend some time with my mother."

As he should. Jaslene tried not to melt even more for him, at his softening toward his family. She even began to think he'd never actually been hardened. He'd only closed himself off, when all the while underneath was the capacity for love. Maybe there was hope for him after all.

"And then we need to get back to Chesterville," Cal said.

Jaslene sobered. They had to go back but they would go back to Riley trying to find a way to make her pay for his perceived wrong.

Jaslene rode with Skylar in her big blue diesel pickup truck along the narrow paved road toward the stable. About a quarter mile from the house, it was an enormous structure with a green metal roof. Miles of fence rose and dipped with the rolling landscape. Trees followed a meandering stream in the valley to the left and horses grazed on hay bales and grass.

"This is our main stable," Skylar said as they walked toward the expansive building. "There are two other barns on the property that you can't see from here." She stopped before entering a side door and pointed toward another sizable building. "That's an indoor riding arena. The others are a carriage house, storage shed and equipment garage. We even have a chicken coop."

"Do you use that greenhouse?"

"Yes. One of our cooks does. He's quite a chef. There's an apple orchard, a pumpkin patch, and behind the house a garden with a path and a pond. It's beautiful in the summer."

That was one thing Cal's house in Chesterville didn't have—a garden. She imagined gardening with him as a couple. Maybe even starting a family.

Seeing several ranch hands moving around the buildings, she could appreciate the amount of work it would take to run a ranch this size. "What other animals do you have besides horses?"

"Some cattle. Goats. Pigs. It brings in a decent revenue. Enough to keep the ranch in the black." She smiled, full of triumph.

Jaslene could see Skylar prided herself at managing the ranch successfully enough not to have to rely on her father's substantial income.

For someone who grew up among all this wealth, Skylar sure did seem humble. She explained everything as information only, with no hint of boasting.

Following her into the stable, she saw that two horses had already been saddled. Skylar must have had this planned long before she'd invited Jaslene to join her.

"Have you ever ridden before?"

"A few times." She was no equestrian but she could stay seated.

Skylar handed her the reins to a brown-and-white horse while she took the big, gray gelding.

"This is Prince Bogie. Bogie for short. He's my baby."

The horse nickered as though protesting the nicknames.

"Bogie, as in Humphrey Bogart?" Jaslene asked.

"My Bogie is a gent." Skylar rubbed the horse's nose.

Outside the stable, Jaslene mounted her paint, hoping she wasn't too rusty to ride with a pro.

"So what's your story, Jaslene?" Skylar asked as they started toward the other buildings.

"What do you want to know?"

"Cal's helping you with the disappearance of your friend. I know you're a geologist and come from a good family. But what about you? What are you looking for in life? I don't see a ring. You never married?"

"My husband died."

"Oh. Cal didn't tell me. I'm sorry."

"It's all right." No one had ever asked her what she was looking for in life. Before college the big question had been what would she do. She hadn't planned marriage, only her education. She'd always figured the rest would just happen.

Now that Ryan was dead, what did she want for her future? "I always did want a family," she said aloud.

"So did Cal."

Jaslene already knew that. Did it matter anymore, though? Could he ever open himself up enough to trust again?

"You asked what I'm looking for in my future. Well, I can tell you one thing. It isn't to be with a man who can never trust me."

Skylar rode for a while without comment. Then at last she said, "Then it looks like Cal will have to learn how to trust again."

Jaslene would not hold on to hope for that.

"You know, Cal's withdrawal from this family started long before he married that woman and moved to Chesterville," Skylar said.

Why did Jaslene get the feeling Skylar was trying to convince her not to give up on Cal?

"It began when our grandfather died. Cal never really related to Dad, as I'm sure you've seen. Corbin… well, Corbin is just Corbin, but me and Mom never butted heads with Cal. Looking back, I guess we didn't talk much to each other, either. Cal drifted off on his own more and more. He joined the rangers and that was it. No more Cal. It hurt Mom the most. She never understood why he left and never came back."

"Cal said she had the same attitude as his dad and brother. He didn't really say that about you, though."

"I feel like I hardly know my brother now. How could he possibly know me?"

That was so sad.

"That doesn't seem fair. Do you think he really meant to abandon your mother?"

"I don't think he thought of it that way. He needed to escape his grief and that led to him alienating himself from anyone who wasn't his grandfather. No one compared to him in Cal's eyes. He loved him that much."

That made sense. "I heard him talking with his dad this morning. They made amends. At least, the beginnings of it."

Skylar nodded and looked ahead as she rode her beautiful horse. "And now he's talking to Mom. I doubt either one of them will have a dry eye."

That wasn't a bad thing. Cal needed to overcome the baggage of his past. Before talking to Skylar, she would have said there was no way she would wait for him. But now...

Cal had a lot on his mind after his talk with his mom. He also had a call with a detective he used to work with, who told him Riley had been spotted in town but had gotten away. It would have been nice to have him captured before he and Jaslene returned.

He sat in the family room waiting for Jaslene to finish washing up after her day with Skylar. The cook was busy in the kitchen preparing dinner. He could hear her clanking around in there and smelled something delicious in the oven.

His mother had accurately assessed that he'd held a lot against his father after his grandfather died. He'd felt disconnected from his family, like he didn't fit in, which had led him to conclude all they cared about was wealth. He still believed that called to his father and brother, but he'd been wrong to extend that label to his mother and sister. His mother had artfully enlightened him during their talk.

Most of what she'd said he'd already known, deep down. His wife had been an excuse to move away from Texas and his family. Hell, he may have even married her in haste to accomplish just that. His marriage had been wrong from the beginning. He had wanted a family, but he probably shouldn't have rushed into a commitment.

His mother had reminded him of an argument he

and his father had, the one right before he'd proposed to his ex-wife.

His father had confronted him on how much he'd withdrawn after Grandfather died. For months he'd avoided spending time with his family, didn't return calls. He'd gone home for the holidays and that's when his father had ushered him into the library.

You never appreciated him, Cal had yelled once the heated conversation had escalated.

All you ever cared about is this. He'd shoved his hands up to indicate the elaborate room.

That's always been your problem, Cal. You care too little about making a good living. You think I do this for myself but you're wrong. I do this to provide security for my family.

It's too excessive. We don't need all of this.

His father had pointed in his face, growing angrier as he always did when Cal spoke his mind. *I believe in working hard. You should learn from my example.*

I don't need to be a millionaire, and you should learn from my example.

What do you want me to do? Give all my money away to those who don't pay their own way?

That had dug deep into his soul. *No*, he'd all but spat. *I don't expect you to ever change. I expect you to be a greedy bastard until the day you die. You've poisoned this family.* Cal had stormed out of the library and left without saying goodbye to anyone.

His brother had relished the rift between Cal and their father, now being the favored son.

After being home for such a short time and talking

with his dad, he realized things had changed. New-man had changed. He still enjoyed a rich lifestyle but he seemed more open-minded now. Maybe Francesca had done that. She must have talked with Newman about how he treated Cal.

Hearing Jaslene come down the stairs, he stood and left the family room. Seeing her in a jean skirt with a soft white three-quarter-sleeved top, boots, and freshly washed and shiny hair, he stopped in the entry of the dining room and just took in the vision of her. She smiled, making his growing feelings for her more dif-ficult to bear. He felt like he was being carried along, toward a certain and painful end. He wished they were already back in Chesterville so he could delve back into the case.

"Is your mother joining us?"

"I don't know." Skylar said she'd come back for dinner and his father had asked if they'd be here to-night. He had often said he'd be home for dinner but rarely ever had.

Seeing the cook had set the table, he took Jaslene's hand. "Come on. Let's have some wine before Dad and Skylar get here." He led her into the family room, where a bar and pool table took up one side, a large television screen and seating area the other. Behind the bar, a wine cellar with glass panels halfway up prom-ised a fine selection.

When he brought out a bottle, Jaslene said, "Just water for me."

He poured her filtered water over ice and put it on the bar, lifting his glass of wine for a sip.

"How did your talk with your mother go?"

His thoughts were still too raw to get into that right now. "It went well."

He saw her register his reluctance. "Are you going to come and see your family more often?"

"Yes."

She sat on a stool, putting down the water. "I like Skylar. She's not what I expected."

"You expected more of the same as my father?" He strolled around the bar and came to stand next to her.

"Based on what you told me, yes."

"She was never the reason I stayed away."

"I know." She ran her forefinger down his chest with a sly grin. "I'm glad you finally realize that."

He felt shallow for allowing the death of his grandfather to do that to people he had no intention of hurting. And he still wasn't sure he would become close to his family again. Visits, sure, but he didn't want to be the only one trying. He wouldn't compromise himself to accommodate them and he just didn't see them getting along as a result. His brother needed to feel superior and his father had been the same, up until his mother had to go to the hospital. Would that last? Had his father really had a life-altering epiphany?

If he showed up on time for dinner, that would be a first step.

"Maybe this trip will give you new insight into what family is supposed to be."

He recoiled, an involuntary, defensive reaction he'd grown accustomed to. He'd grown accustomed to his strict thoughts on women and what they would do to his hopes. He'd figured the right woman would have to prove her trustworthiness. After all, he thought he'd had a family with his ex-wife. After she betrayed him he'd realized he'd never been shown what that kind of family should be. He didn't feel he had that with his own, not back then. Now…that remained to be seen.

"Maybe it's giving *you* some insight," he said.

He became annoyed because her past heartbreak gave her equal reason not to trust. Did she expect him to be the first to open up in whatever this was going on between them? She seemed to want him to soften toward his family so that he'd soften his defenses toward her. What if he did and *she* ended up being the one to run?

No thanks. "Shall we go to the dining room?"

She stood from the stool, leaving her half-finished water.

The front door opened and he heard Skylar's loud "Whoa. Dang, it's cold out there for Texas."

"Wimp," Cal teased.

"It's just a little bit colder in West Virginia this time of year."

"It's the South here."

Skylar stepped toward them with a smile. "Hey, I don't like cold. I'm a Texan for a reason."

"Global warming is your friend."

She laughed and leaned in for a hug. "I'm so glad you decided to come home." Leaning back she added, "And I love your girlfriend. I think you should marry her." She bent a knee as she tippy-toed to kiss his cheek.

Cal looked at Jaslene, who feigned nonchalance.

"I forgot how much I adore you," he said to Skylar.

Skylar looked around, seemingly oblivious to Cal's sarcasm. "I thought Dad was joining us. I would have stayed home otherwise."

"I stayed to see if he would, too." Cal ignored how Jaslene eyed him, as though he should have more faith in his family.

Skylar laughed. "He's mellowed out since you stopped coming around. His only fault was working too much, but I do think that's about to change." They went into the dining room, where the table was almost ready.

"He's also getting older," Skylar said, sitting on the end of the long side of the table. "He might even retire."

"Has he told you that?" Cal sat beside Jaslene and opposite his sister. He had a hard time believing his father would ever retire.

"No."

The cook put a salad on the table. The salmon next to it smelled delicious but the baked potatoes were nothing spectacular. This was all healthy.

"Is Mom coming down for dinner?" he asked the cook.

"Yes, sir."

He wasn't used to being called "sir" in the last few years. "I'll go and get her." He started to rise.

"No need. Her home nurse will bring her. She's on her way now." The cook left the dining area as Cal sat back down on his chair.

His father appeared in the dining room. He must have entered through the garage.

"Look who made it!" Skylar exclaimed, voicing how Cal felt.

His father had actually made it home for dinner. He watched him remove his jacket and hang it over the back of a chair, taking the seat next to his daughter.

"Of course I did." Newman smiled over at Cal, who turned when he heard his mother enter.

"I can walk on my own." His mother tried to shrug off the help of the nurse. "I had a minor stroke, not a major one. I can talk, can't I?"

"I've got her from here," he said. "Go and enjoy the rest of your night."

Cal had never seen his dad so friendly with employees. The nurse thanked him and left with a spreading smile.

"How are you feeling, Mother?" Cal asked. "You seem to have your strength back."

"I never lost my strength. I'm glad to see you're still here." Francesca checked out the meal. "I'm famished. This looks like stroke victim food."

"Low sodium and heart healthy," Newman said. "Doctor's orders."

She grimaced and reached for the utensil on the salmon platter. Newman brushed her hand away and scooped up a filet for her.

Cal waited for Skylar and Jaslene to begin filling their plates, content to watch his father dote on his mother. Although she sent Newman an annoyed look, Cal could tell her eyes also conveyed love. He was glad he'd come on this trip. How it would change his future relations with his family, he didn't feel like examining just yet. For now, he'd just enjoy being with them without any conflict. He'd also enjoy Jaslene being with him, though he was reluctant to admit she felt like part of the family, too.

She was about to take her first bite when her eyes connected with his and softened with affection. He wasn't sure if she sensed how he felt, but he had a pretty good idea she did.

Growing uncomfortable over the warm connection building in this moment, he finished filling his plate. As he picked up his fork and took a bite of salmon, he caught Skylar watching him with her sharp eyes, eyes that twinkled with approval.

"Newman said you plan to go home tomorrow, Cal," Francesca said.

Cal nodded. "We fly back in the morning." They had been gone three days and it felt much longer than that. What would they go back to and how far would he have to go to protect Jaslene?

Chapter 10

After picking up Rapunzel, Jaslene and Cal returned to his house. She had just finished unpacking and was ready to relax with a cup of tea when the doorbell rang. Still in the jeans and black sweater she'd worn on the flight home, she walked in stockinged feet downstairs. Cal had opened the door to allow a woman inside. In a warm winter jacket and blue-gray pants that looked like they went with a uniform, the woman pushed back the hood of the jacket to reveal brown hair in a pony-tail. Her brown eyes and the set of her mouth were tense. Whatever had brought her here must have her anxious: it must be about Payton.

"Jaslene, this is Bonita Lawrence. She's a nurse for Dr. Benjamin."

A shock wave zapped her before she quickly recovered and realized this could mean a big break in the case.

"*Was* a nurse for Dr. Benjamin," the woman corrected. "I got your address from the police station. I hope you don't mind me stopping by."

"Not at all. Why don't we go somewhere more comfortable and talk?" Cal said. "Can I take your jacket?"

While Cal took it to a new coatrack in the entry and hung it up, Jaslene led the woman into the living room and then went to the kitchen to get some refreshments. When she returned to the living room, Cal had engaged Bonita in casual talk, which evidently did little to calm her.

Jaslene put down the water.

Bonita looked up at her. "Do you have anything stronger?"

She obviously needed something to take the edge off. Jaslene grew hopeful that she'd reveal something to move the case forward.

"Whiskey?"

"With a splash of soda, if you have it."

Cal went to a cabinet and opened it to reveal a small bar. He prepared the drink.

"How long did you work for Dr. Benjamin?" Jaslene asked.

"Many years."

She only seemed capable of short responses right now. Cal returned and handed Bonita the drink. She took it and drank a long sip without any trace of a grimace, then cradled the glass in her hands.

"I heard you came by and talked to Dr. Benjamin

about Payton Everett and he said he never had an affair with her."

"Yes," Cal said.

Jaslene could tell he didn't push because, like her, he sensed this could be significant.

"He did have an affair with her. Payton came in a few times and I was her nurse. We talked. She said she was going to lunch with him after her appointment and he was taking the afternoon off so they could spend some time together. I followed them to a hotel and took pictures in case I ever needed it. Turns out I was too scared to use it, but now…"

Jaslene glanced at Cal at this but he remained focused on the woman. He took a photo from her. It was Dr. Benjamin and Payton going into a hotel.

"His receptionist said she made reservations for that day and many others. He must have met Payton on many occasions."

"What day was that? Do you remember?"

"Yes. It was a week before she was reported missing."

That meant Payton had been seeing him right up until she disappeared.

"Why are you telling us this now?" Cal asked.

"He fired me a few days ago. I never did like him. Something about him bothered me, like you couldn't trust a single thing he said. He came across as friendly and charming, but he'd often make promises he never kept. I asked for a raise three times and he agreed but I never did get one. He was nice to patients but if they were poor or not very smart, he'd talk about them after they left. His having an affair with a patient bothered me, too. Doctors aren't supposed to do that sort of thing. He didn't seem to care what anyone thought. In fact, he acted like he could do whatever he wanted and no one could stop him."

Jaslene had gotten the same impression about Dr. Benjamin. She indicated her uniform. "It looks like you're still working."

"I work for a home health organization now, one that competes with Dr. Benjamin's. They picked me up the day after he fired me."

"Did you notice anything strange after Payton's disappearance?" Cal asked. "Any change in Dr. Benjamin's behavior?"

"No. Not really. He didn't seem very troubled that his mistress had gone missing. I thought that was very strange."

"Why did he fire you?" Jaslene asked.

"I saw him getting too close to another patient. He thought he was alone with a beautiful woman who seemed to not mind his attention. When he confronted me later, he asked if I would say anything to anyone. All I told him is what he did was wrong and not to speak to me about it again. From then on, he reprimanded me for every little thing he perceived as a mistake until about a week later he fired me."

"Did you tell anyone?" Cal asked.

"His receptionist, but she already knew what he was like. She didn't seem to mind working for a pig, but I did."

Jaslene could not reconcile the Payton she knew

with one who would fall for an unscrupulous man. "Did you always think Dr. Benjamin was a pig?" she asked.

Bonita shook her head. "When I first started working for him he seemed to genuinely care about his employees, his patients, too. Like I said, he could be charming. Only after time did I begin to see that was all a facade."

"Can you give us some examples?"

"He would sometimes lose his temper with the staff, especially if the day grew long, or if he had to treat a difficult patient, someone demanding or with a complicated medical condition. He'd snap at us all and throw things. Another time I saw him with another doctor who disagreed with his diagnosis. I've never seen Dr. Benjamin more chilling. He didn't lose his temper, but he put the doctor in his place—even though he was probably wrong."

"Did Payton ever know of any of these types of instances?" Cal asked.

"Not that I know of."

What if she had? What if she'd noticed a lot more than that? Payton, being a reporter, could have stumbled onto something that Dr. Benjamin preferred to keep secret—like a bad diagnosis that caused someone harm or death. Then again, just because he was a jerk didn't mean he was capable of kidnapping or murder.

Later that day, Cal stepped into The Sunflower with Jaslene. They hadn't talked much about their trip to

Texas since returning, other than Jaslene expressing how much she liked Skylar.

His talks with Mother had been difficult. With her brush with death she'd been candid about his lengthy absence. By the time she finished telling him how much she'd missed him and that she didn't understand why he refused to come and see her, he felt terrible. Of course, she'd correctly attributed it to his father, but she had scolded him for making her wait until she was hospitalized to visit. His mother's opening up had been a first—and it had been enough.

She had effectively instilled a good amount of guilt and made him promise not to stay away so long again.

He hadn't expected his trip to have such a positive outcome, mostly attributed to Jaslene.

The hostess went to get the general manager. Cal waited beside Jaslene, who had worn a sweater dress that hugged her body and had him reminiscing on things best left alone.

The general manager, a lanky man in black dress pants and a gray-pin-striped white shirt and dark tie, approached. His dark brown hair was neatly trimmed, his gray eyes had dark circles beneath and he smiled as though weary.

"Gary Sherman." He held out his hand. Cal shook it first, then Jaslene.

"Thanks for seeing us." Cal took out a photo of Payton and handed it to the man. "Do you recognize this woman?"

"No, but I don't interface with customers as much as the waitstaff. When was she last in?"

Cal gave him the date.

"Hang tight, I'll look and see who worked that day."

Cal waited with Jaslene a few minutes before the GM returned. "Three of the four waitresses are here today."

"Perfect. Can we talk to them one at a time?"

"Certainly." He turned to the hostess. "Why don't you seat them in a booth."

The first waitress didn't recall seeing or waiting on Dr. Benjamin and Payton. The second did. A blonde twentysomething college student said, "Dr. Benjamin comes in here a lot. Most of the time he's by himself or with a colleague, but I did notice him bring in that woman." She pointed to the photograph of Benjamin and Payton that Cal had shown her and placed on the table. "They sat close and he kept leaning toward her in a way that suggested they were a couple."

Cal inwardly cheered her keen observation. "How often did he bring her here?"

"Probably three or four times over about a four-month period."

"Do you remember the last time they were in?"

The girl thought a moment. "It was a Tuesday, my last day of work before I planned to drive to see my parents for the weekend."

That was just days before Payton had gone missing. "Did you notice anything unusual about them?"

"Not really. They seemed quieter than usual. She didn't seem to say much to him and didn't smile and laugh like she normally did."

Had something brought on that change? "Can we get records of the payment transactions?" Cal asked.

"I'll ask the manager."

The next waitress came over. An older woman with curly, dark red hair and tired hazel eyes sat across from them.

Cal showed her the photo. "Do you recognize the woman in this picture?"

Beside him Jaslene quietly watched and listened.

The waitress leaned over and squinted.

Cal didn't harbor much hope this woman would remember anything more than the previous waitress about serving Payton and the doctor. She continued to study the picture. Then she picked it up off the table and held it close to her face.

"Yes, I remember them. They came in for dinner a lot, but it has been a long, long time since then. I remember one night last… May, I think it was. He complained about the wine and then sent his plate back twice." She put down the picture. "He wasn't a nice man. He usually is demanding when he comes in. None of us like to serve him. I haven't seen him with that woman in a long time, but I remember her because she got a little tipsy that night. They seemed to like each other."

Cal thanked her and decided to leave. All they had heard today was that Dr. Benjamin probably hadn't done anything nefarious or possibly sexual with Payton. Once again, after following this lead for so long, they had come to a frustrating dead end.

* * *

Jaslene and Cal next went to Dr. Benjamin's clinic.

Inside the doctor's modern, earth-toned waiting room, they stepped in line behind two patients.

"We're here to talk to Dr. Benjamin," Cal said to the receptionist when it was their turn.

"Do you have an appointment?"

"No. Tell him Cal Chelsey is here to see him."

The receptionist put down her pen and looked harried. "He's very busy, Mr. Chelsey. He won't be able to see you today."

"He'll see us. Tell him we need to speak with him about Payton Everett and that if he doesn't talk to us, he'll have to talk to police."

That smoothed her expression. "Just a moment."

Jaslene waited with Cal at the desk. About five minutes later, the receptionist returned. "His nurse will be up to get you."

About a minute later a nurse appeared from a hallway. "Mr. Chelsey?"

"Yes."

"Follow me."

Jaslene trailed behind Cal down the hallway to an office entrance. "He'll be in as soon as he can."

Entering the familiar office with the view of forested foothills, Jaslene sat next to Cal on one of two blue chairs facing the tidy desk. The electronic photo frame flashed pictures of people that were probably the doctor's wife and kids.

Jaslene found it quite distasteful that the doctor

would display his family like that with all his running-around with other women. Did he only have it there for show?

"He's going to make us wait in here a while," she said.

"Maybe he hopes we'll give up and leave." He stood and moved to the other side of the desk.

She watched him riffle through a neat stack of papers that looked like the doctor's mail. He glanced through the first few and spent more time on the fifth.

"American Express bill," he said. "Still going to The Sunflower."

Jaslene looked back at the closed door and faced him again. "Nothing else?"

He finished going through the stack and then wiggled the mouse. "Password."

Returning to the chair opposite the desk, he sat just as Dr. Benjamin entered the office.

"Sorry to keep you waiting." He moved behind his desk and sat. "I have a lot of patients with colds and the flu."

"We have time," Cal said, clearly intimating the doctor wasn't getting rid of them.

"What do you want to talk to me about Payton?" he asked. "I've told you all I can."

"Maybe, but not all you should have." Cal slid a copy of the last transaction the restaurant had provided them. "This is proof you were at The Sunflower just days before Payton Everett went missing."

The doctor looked it over and then lifted his head, untroubled. "So? I go there a lot."

"More than one waitress identified you with Payton. One of them can put you there with her the week she went missing."

Benjamin stared at them with unflinching eyes. "I don't understand. If I had lunch with Payton, that doesn't implicate me in her disappearance."

"It was dinner, and the waitress said you were close to Payton, that you were a couple."

Dr. Benjamin stared again; only now his armor began to slip. He blinked once and let out a long sigh. "All right. I did have an affair with her, but she ended it because I was married. She gave up on me."

Jaslene could hardly contain her excitement. Would they actually get a break and find out what happened to Payton?

"Why did you lie to us the last time we were here?" Cal asked.

Dr. Benjamin smirked. "That should be obvious. I didn't want my wife to find out. Payton is missing. If she finds out I'm being questioned about that, she'll know I had an affair. There is also the professional misconduct to consider."

"Isn't it more important to find Payton?" Jaslene asked. "What if she's still alive?"

"There's nothing I can offer you that would help find her. The last time I saw her was two days before, when we had dinner at The Sunflower. She broke things off with me that night."

That corroborated with what the young waitress had said. Payton hadn't been very talkative and he had been more subdued than usual. Had she just gotten tired of seeing a married man or had she discovered something else that had caused the change in her behavior?

"Did you have any feelings for her when you were seeing her?"

The doctor's brow lowered as though a strong reaction had compelled him. "Of course. I was very attracted to her physically, and I enjoyed her energy. I can't say I was impressed with her profession as a reporter, but she did have an intelligent mind."

He spoke as though he considered her mediocre except for her body. Jaslene was disgusted. What had Payton seen in this guy? She must have discovered he wasn't all he seemed later on.

"Why weren't you impressed with her profession?" Cal asked, seeming neutral. But Jaslene knew he had his detective hat on.

"Reporters look for stories."

"Payton wanted to write more investigative pieces," Jaslene said. "Did you know that about her?"

He shook his head. "No. She never mentioned that." He held up his hands. "Don't get me wrong. I respected Payton and I liked being with her."

"But it didn't bother you in the least that she broke up with you?" Cal asked.

His mouth pursed slightly, as though the reminder stung. "It bothered me. I didn't want to stop seeing her, but like I said before, I respected her decision."

"That must happen to you a lot," Jaslene said. The good doctor must expect his mistresses to break off their affairs with him because he clearly had no intention of leaving his wife.

"How did you feel about her ending your relationship?" Cal asked with a warning look at her.

"I expected it," the doctor said, confirming her assessment. "I knew it bothered her that I was married, and the night we had dinner I told her I couldn't leave my wife and kids. As strange as it sounds, I still love my wife. Aside from that, I won't put my kids into a broken home living situation. Payton understood that at first but when she realized she could never have me, she walked away. I had no hard feelings. I missed her. I liked her quite a bit. She was smart and witty and attractive. I enjoyed being with her."

"But you still love your wife." Jaslene found that difficult to believe. "Normally people don't betray the ones they love." When presented with the choice between passion and respect for the man she married, she had chosen the latter. She had loved Ryan as a best friend.

"I love my wife for different reasons than those that drew me to Payton. My wife is sophisticated and soft-spoken. She's a good mother. She's everything I've always wanted in a wife."

He sounded as though he wanted a woman to fill a role to complement his successful career.

"How much did Payton know about your practice, Dr. Benjamin?"

Jaslene wondered why he'd asked such a question. Was he fishing for a motive?

The doctor didn't falter. "I'm not sure I follow. I was her primary care physician. She learned of me when she did an article on the success of my practice and all it has to offer."

Cal waved his hand through the air. "Four clinics and two home health care services. You have quite a presence."

"Maybe she found something when she was researching for the article," Jaslene said.

"Are you hoping I have some kind of secret to hide?" The doctor chuckled. "I am afraid I am much more boring than that."

Or not.

Cal stood. "Thank you for seeing us." He waited for Jaslene to stand with him. "We'll be in touch if we have any more questions for you."

"I have nothing to hide," the doctor said.

"We'll see," Cal replied.

"If you have more questions, you're going to have to talk to my lawyer from now on." He stood from behind his desk. "I'm sure you can understand I'm not comfortable with what you've insinuated here today. I had nothing to do with Payton's disappearance, but you seem determined to make everyone believe I did."

Jaslene stopped with Cal at the door as he paused to look back at Dr. Benjamin. "I don't care what anyone believes, Doctor. I only care about the truth. And the missing person in this case."

Before walking away with Cal, Jaslene saw the doctor's frown of displeasure. He didn't like his character being dragged through the mud. Did he have a good reason to feel offended or had he lied when he said he had nothing to hide?

Chapter 11

A cold front brought blustering snow on this mid-February day. They were having a colder than usual winter this year. Cal walked with Jaslene toward a diner. Several days had passed with no new leads. Cal had placed surveillance on Dr. Benjamin, who kept to a routine. He behaved like a normal family man: home every night for dinner, no secret meetings with women or patients.

Riley seemed to have vanished for good. He must be using cash and had no presence on social media. They had searched the town in an attempt to locate him and met with no success. He'd likely fled and now used an alias. No one had seen him or his motorcycle. Cal, with Jaslene in tow, made regular visits to restaurants, gas stations, and motels and hotels. He was convinced

Riley found a hiding place outside of town, but eventually he'd return. Resentment would be his magnet. He wouldn't be able to stay away if he craved vengeance.

Each man carried their own level of suspicion. Dr. Benjamin might be covering his tracks. Riley running carried a message of guilt. Both had motives but Cal had no evidence that would conclusively produce an arrest. Cal held the door of the diner open for Jaslene, who ducked her head away from spitting snow. Stomping his feet on the damp entry rug, he waited for the hostess to greet them and take them to their table.

He watched Jaslene remove her jacket and let it hang over the back of the chair. Her skinny jeans had already captured his attention after his first glimpse of her this morning. Strands of thick, golden-blond hair slipped down off her shoulder but caught by the edge of the scarf as she moved.

Settled in the chair, she reached for the menu and caught him watching her. Her eyes, a shade darker than his, found his and stayed with them.

"What?" She wiped her face. "Is something wrong?"

"No." Quite the contrary. "You're beautiful."

Her hand stilled and she went stiff with what he surmised was surprise.

She lowered her menu. "So are you."

That he hadn't expected. He chuckled. "Are you saying I'm pretty?"

Smiling she shook her head. "No. You're much too rugged to be pretty. *Handsome* doesn't quite cover it, either." She surveyed his face unabashedly. "*Hot* is better."

Okay, he'd rather not have this conversation. But he had to ask, "You think I'm hot?"

"Yes."

"I might have believed you when I was thirty."

"You're not that old."

Thirty-seven wasn't old but there'd been a time he'd thought he'd be deep into family life by now.

The waiter arrived and took their order.

"How many men have told you you're beautiful?" Cal didn't know why he had to ask but he had the whim to.

"Not many." She paused as she thought. "Ryan never told me I was beautiful. He just said he loved me."

She seemed to ponder that revelation, falling into a somber mood.

"There had to be men after Ryan died. He died what, two years ago?"

"Yes." She still seemed somber, as though the idea of her dating other men bothered her. Why? Out of guilt?

"Men had to have hit on you in that time. Why didn't you date any?" he asked, more curious than ever.

"It took me a while to get over Ryan's death. I'm still not really over it."

She'd already told him she felt like she'd be betraying her husband if she saw other men. Had she drawn the same conclusion with him? Maybe her guilt over her passion for her colleague would keep her faithful to a dead husband.

"How many men hit on you?" he asked.

"I don't know. A couple. Another geologist and someone I met through a client." She fingered the napkin wrapped around a knife and fork.

"Another scientist asked you out on a date?" he asked, feeling a little jealous.

"We were working a contract with a corporation interested in using wind and solar energy alternatives. The project took several weeks. We stayed at the same hotel, so we shared meals together. He asked if I'd go out with him when we got home. I explained about Ryan and he said to keep him in mind when I was ready."

"And did you?"

She considered him a moment. "Why are you so curious?"

"Did you keep the geologist in mind?"

She breathed a laugh. "No. Not beyond him being a coworker. I wouldn't have been interested in him anyway."

"Why not?"

"He was too much like me, I guess. And…" Her eyes moved over the restaurant as she thought. "Too nerdy."

She didn't like nerds, huh? He was definitely no nerd. He grinned, seeing how she noticed.

"Why are you so curious?" she asked again.

"I'm trying to determine what I'm up against." Would she ever be free of her guilt?

"Are you asking if I'm ready to start dating again?"

He waited, trying to tell her without words that he

was. Being with his family again seemed to have re-awakened him but he felt like a bumbling idiot right now.

She turned away, looking across the restaurant at other patrons as she thought. Cal became aware of muffled conversation, dishes clanking and staff moving about serving customers.

At last she faced him again. "I think being with you might help me."

Help her. How? Was he some kind of transition? He hated this uncertainty. It made him feel weak and bolstered his resistance to dating.

"I don't feel bad being with you," she said.

What if she just said that to try to win his trust? Why would she do that? His family had a lot of money; maybe she had her sights on an inheritance.

He sounded paranoid in his own head. He was falling hard for her.

"I'm just not sure I'm ready for another serious relationship," she said.

While her honesty again didn't go unnoticed, he wondered if he'd wind up hurt anyway. She wouldn't have to betray him. She could simply walk away because she wasn't ready to move on. The possibility of rejection didn't settle well with him.

"It isn't as though we chose each other," he said.

She smiled slightly. "True."

Neither of them had consciously sought the other out with the intention of dating. Their intimacy had happened on its own.

He spotted their waiter, who had just then retrieved their plates and left the kitchen. Reaching the table, he set their plates down and looked at Cal. Then he glanced at Jaslene. Cal didn't think he was wary over his tardiness in delivering their food. He seemed to have thought of something or maybe recognized one of them.

The waiter straightened after putting down the plates and contemplated Cal. "You that PI who's looking for Riley Sawyer?"

"Yes?" Cal's anticipation soared.

"A guy came in the other day. He was passing through and read the local paper that had an article about Riley. He said he stopped for gas in Webster Springs on his way back from Snowshoe and saw a man who fit Riley's description filling a motorcycle with gas. It struck him as odd because it's February and cold."

Webster Springs. "Did you get a name?"

"No and he paid cash. Sorry. I told him he should go to police and he seemed like he would. Didn't he?"

"No. When was that?" Cal asked.

"Oh." His eyes lifted as he thought. "Three days ago."

Three days. Riley could be anywhere by now.

When the waiter left, Jaslene faced him with brighter eyes. "We should expand our search to other towns."

"Starting with Webster Springs."

Webster Springs was about fifteen miles from Chesterville. "Riley might be gone already."

"Not if he feels safe there. He probably didn't see that man notice him."

"That's what we hope for, but in case he's moving from place to place…"

"We will check every town."

This time when she smiled she conveyed something other than romantic flirtation. She appreciated his determination to solve her missing friend's case.

Jaslene drove with Cal through Webster Springs to the outskirts of town. They'd found that gas station where Riley also regularly stopped for gas or cigarettes. The attendant even told them where Riley was staying, having seen him one day as he passed by. Their luck had finally improved.

Arriving in the motel parking lot, she spotted Riley's motorcycle parked outside a lower level room with an outdoor entrance.

"You stay back," Cal said as they neared.

She stopped far enough away to be safe but still see Cal. He knocked on the motel room door. After a few seconds, he tried to peer into the single front window.

Drawing his gun, he glanced at her and said, "Stay here," and ran toward the side of the motel.

Alert and ready to run if need be, Jaslene went to Riley's motorcycle and unbuckled one of the side storage bags. Nothing was in the right rear bag and the left was also empty. She hadn't expected to find anything of value, but still looked for anything that could link him to Payton. Hearing sudden rapid footfalls, she looked up and saw Riley running toward her—toward his bike. Just as she straightened and would have moved out of the way, he reached her, grabbing her arm and throwing her aside.

She landed painfully on the concrete, on her hip,

elbow and hands. Luckily she wore gloves and a winter jacket, but the hard pavement still dug into her hip.

Cal ran toward them as Riley revved his bike and started to back it up. Seeing she was in his way, she rolled to the side as he backed away from the parking space and swung the bike into a skidding curve.

Cal reached her, crouching before her. "Are you all right?"

"Yes." She scrambled to her feet with Cal helping and ran with him to his SUV. But by the time they raced into the street, the bike was out of sight.

Cal cursed and pounded the steering wheel once.

Jaslene would have done the same if she'd had one in front of her.

They returned to the motel, climbing into the room through the bathroom window, which was how Riley had escaped. He'd left his clothes and a mess but it took them minutes to go through his suitcase. He had receipts on the TV counter, one from a coffee shop in Chesterville.

"He's been going to Chesterville," Cal said.

"And renting adult movies." She held up a motel receipt that included a list of charges.

Cal took it. "He must have planned to check out today."

That meant he was on the move, trying to avoid capture. "For someone who knows the police have no evidence to arrest him, he sure acts guilty."

The case stalled again. Days passed and no sign of Riley. She and Cal drove to Webster Springs every day, searching for him. He had likely gone to another town. Cal had contacted every law enforcement office in the surrounding cities and towns, but no word had come of Riley's whereabouts.

Jaslene had to work on her frustration. Would they ever catch whomever was responsible for Payton's disappearance? Would Jaslene ever know what had become of her friend? She wouldn't quit until Payton was found, but what if they never learned anything new? What if eventually even Cal gave up? How long could they keep this up? Not forever. Jaslene would have to go back to work and Cal would have to take on other cases.

Sitting with a cup of tea, her legs curled up on a wingback chair in the family room, she watched snow flutter down in the fading afternoon light. Rapunzel lay curled in her lap and she stroked her soft, sleeping head.

A faint odor tickled her nose. She went still, thinking she smelled smoke. Then she heard the fire alarm. Propelled into action mode, she stood and put Rapunzel on the chair and walked from the family room into the kitchen; smoke floated, thicker and thicker, toward her.

"Oh my God!" Where was Cal?

Just as she turned to go get Rapunzel and get out of the house, a shape appeared to her side and hit her over the head with something hard. Everything went black.

Cal heard yipping from downstairs as he emerged from the walk-in closet fully dressed after his shower.

The shrill scream of fire alarms a second later had him grabbing his pistol from the nightstand and running from the bedroom before buttoning up his shirt. As soon as he entered the hallway, a man appeared at the top of the stairs wearing a ski mask and aiming a gun. Cal had just enough time to register that the intruder looked to be about the same size as Riley and not as tall as Dr. Benjamin, before Cal ducked into the next bedroom and the first gunshot rang out.

He quickly poked his head into the hallway and shot back. The man had begun to walk down the hall toward him as though he meant to kill Cal and leave him and Jaslene in the house to burn. The man flinched as a bullet from Cal's gun hit him in the leg. From all he could see in the fleeting time he'd stuck his head out into the hall, he'd only grazed the man, who clearly had not expected Cal to be armed. He'd planned to catch him and Jaslene by surprise.

Where is Jaslene?

Cal peered into the hall again and saw the man going back downstairs. With his gun raised, he ran after him. When he reached the stairs, the man turned back and fired. Cal held back at the corner as bullets hit the stairway and the wall across from the top step. When the gunfire paused, he fired back, going down the stairs after the man, who limped as he swung the front door open and fled.

Smoke filled the lower level and he saw flames engulfing the family room.

"Jaslene!" He glanced toward the front door, wanting to go after the man who'd set fire to his house and tried to kill them.

Yipping preceded Rapunzel's running entrance. Swooping the tiny dog up, he covered both their faces with the open lapel of his shirt and saw Jaslene on the floor.

Heat from the fire grew nearly unbearable close to the kitchen.

Coughing, he put Rapunzel down to lift Jaslene into his arms. The dog clawed at his leg.

"Come, Rapunzel!" Cal ran with Jaslene toward the front door, still coughing.

Rapunzel leaped through the open door ahead of him, tearing across the front yard to the sidewalk, where Cal stopped and lowered his head to choke out the smoke that had irritated his throat and lungs.

Cal searched for the masked man but saw nothing but concerned neighbors. He'd gotten away.

Sirens sounded from down the street as Cal lay Jaslene on the front lawn. Brushing hair away from her face, he noticed blood on the sleeve of his shirt where her head had rested as he carried her. Oh no.

Gently he felt her head and found a lump and a gash. Nothing life threatening.

He breathed heavy with relief. "Jaslene." He touched her face.

She moaned.

"Jaslene. Wake up."

Rapunzel appeared at her side, licking her face with a whimper.

Jaslene moaned again and her eyes fluttered open and focused on him. "What happened?"

"You're okay," he said. "Someone set the house on fire."

A fire truck stopped in the street and an ambulance and two police cars weren't far behind.

Cal turned to his house. The living room had gone up in flames and the fire was spreading. He felt a deep and ravaging sense of loss. While he might not have consciously bought this place with having a family in mind, he'd stolen a few moments to entertain those possibilities since Jaslene had been living with him. Now it was gone.

"You can rebuild."

He looked down at Jaslene, who had watched him and accurately ascertained his thoughts.

"In the meantime, you can stay with me at my place."

At first she flustered him with her disarming solution.

"You think I'd let you out of my sight?" he murmured.

A slow smile curved her mouth, soft and full of emotional connection. He felt himself drift into deeper, more undeniable territory, the territory of love. He meant to keep her safe, but his words had dual meaning in this case. He wouldn't let her out of his sight because that was also what his heart clamored for.

Danger brought out his protective and affectionate sides, apparently.

Chapter 12

Sitting at her high, four-seat kitchen table, Jaslene arched her back and twisted left and right. She ached and her stomach was upset. Was she getting sick? It had been a couple of days since the fire and they still didn't know who started it. She had fallen into a domestic routine with Cal at her house. Sleeping together, just cuddling. Having dinner together. Waking in the morning and sharing coffee and the local news. It was so easy talking with him. But underneath the facade of normality was the ever-present uncertainty of where they would end up when all of this chaos ended.

Rubbing her belly, she tried to focus on the book open on her Kindle. Queasiness had woken her just after 2:00 a.m. and she didn't think she was ready to try to go back to bed yet. She almost woke Rapunzel to keep her company, but Punzie looked so adorable sleeping peacefully at Cal's hip that she'd left her.

Jaslene had tried drinking warm milk but that hadn't helped and neither was her attempt at reading. Putting down the Kindle, she looked around her kitchen, noticing how bare it was. Why had she never decorated? She had bought the house after Ryan died, unable to live in the home they'd had together.

She'd been busy with work in the past few years. Home life hadn't worked out so well for her, so maybe she'd given up. Her house was a ten-year-old, modern, two-bedroom ranch. At the time she'd bought the house she hadn't planned on being home much, not wanting to be alone. She worked long hours and spent a lot of time outside or doing other things, going to movies, events in town. That had been a by-product of her failed relationships. She'd decided to just be alone for a while. No more men.

And then Cal had come along. At first, she had considered him no different than other men she encountered in her post-failed-relationship era. Only until he'd left the force and joined DAI had the attraction taken on its own life. She still wasn't sure how she felt about him now. She only knew she didn't want to think about it.

Her stomach churned again, signaling she'd be up a little longer.

Standing, she walked to the den and went to the blue-and-off-white love seat with a soft blue throw draped over the back. She'd picked up the old trunk at a garage sale and it served as her coffee table. She'd also found the paintings hanging on the walls, her favorite cities at night. New York. San Francisco. And smaller unknowns, little towns in the Midwest and Rockies. She had other art depicting places that fascinated her, places with geological features like the Grand Canyon at sunset, folded rock formations in the Wasatch Range and, of course, Yellowstone.

Curling up on the love seat, she turned on the television, thinking maybe her nausea was beginning to subside. Flipping through channels, she checked the weather and news.

Another sudden wave of nausea commandeered her stomach. Jaslene bent over and couldn't suppress a moan. She held her stomach and wondered again why she felt so awful. She didn't have a fever.

What the…

She lifted her head and stared straight ahead at the television without really seeing it. *Nausea…?*

She'd had late periods before but now as she counted, she came to the shocking realization that she was *much* too late. Her breasts had been a little sore. But she hadn't thought to be concerned. Memories of making love crashed upon her.

"What are you doing up?"

Jaslene sucked in a breath when she heard Cal. The sound of his footfalls accompanied his affectionate, deep tone.

"I couldn't sleep." She saw him going to the fridge in the kitchen, sleepy-eyed and in only his boxers. She tried not to look down there or at the rest of his rock-hard body.

"How come?"

"I…don't know." His sexiness took her mind off her nausea.

Taking orange juice out, he turned his head with a half-awake but skeptical look. "Is something bothering you?"

She almost laughed, panicked. Should she tell him or was it premature? She might only have a bug.

"I slept but woke and couldn't go back to sleep," she said.

He poured a glass of juice and put the container back into the refrigerator. Taking a drink, he came into the den, his eyes scanning the room.

Was he going to join her in his underwear?

Jaslene still reeled from wondering if she was actually pregnant. The sight of him in only his underwear was too intimate right now.

"This is a nice room." He sat next to her, holding his glass of juice in one hand and stretching his other arm out behind her.

Awareness of him and the sweet warming as a result vanished as more persistent nausea roiled. Her head began to feel cold and tingles chased down her arms.

"What's the matter?" Cal traced his finger down her face.

"I don't feel well."

His brow lowered a little as he surveyed her. "Why not?"

"I don't know." She put her hand on her forehead and wrapped her arm across her stomach with the other. The nausea intensified.

Jumping up from the love seat, she ran to the nearest bathroom, holding her mouth and barely making it to the toilet.

After several minutes, she finally felt better. She went to the sink and washed her mouth. When she finished, she looked up into the mirror and saw Cal standing in the doorway with an apprehensive question in his eyes.

"It started this morning," she said.

"You are on the Pill, aren't you?"

"I…was…" Before Ryan died, she'd stopped taking them with him and had not gotten pregnant, so she assumed she wasn't a Fertile Myrtle.

Cal stepped farther into the bathroom and banged his fist down onto the counter, making Jaslene gasp and take a step back.

"Why didn't you tell me?"

Angry that he seemed about to blame her, she stepped forward again. "It didn't occur to me until just now. Why didn't you *ask*?"

He instantly regained control of his emotions. He rubbed his forehead above his eyes and then met hers, gravely concerned.

"Why weren't you on the Pill?"

"Why did you assume I was?" she shot back.

"You said it was all right."

"I thought it was. I never got pregnant with Ryan."

He stared at her for long, uncomfortable seconds. "What are we going to do?"

"We don't even know if I'm pregnant yet." Why work themselves into a frenzy? She couldn't even think about having a baby with him. That would be dangerous because she knew right then that she would love it.

He cocked his head at her, clearly not needing a test to convince him. She hadn't yet been able to accept the reality of a baby coming into her life soon.

"I don't know what we're going to do. I'll have the baby and raise it. You can be a part of our lives if that's what you want." She still wasn't sure how she wanted to handle that. Secretly she hoped he would come around and raise the child with her.

"I don't think either one of us will benefit from being forced into parenting," he said.

"Well, we may not have a choice."

"We aren't ready for this."

"No. That's for sure. But what can we do?" She looked pointedly into his eyes so he wouldn't misunderstand her. "I refuse to get an abortion just because you aren't ready." They'd both made this mistake and now they were going to have to deal with the consequences. They both should have thought before they had sex.

"We don't have to get married."

More anger stormed his eyes. She had never seen him this way before.

"What are you suggesting, then? That we share a baby but not live together? I won't pass a child back and forth for eighteen years."

"Well, getting married doesn't have to be the solution, either. I agree with that. Whether we're ready or not doesn't really matter, does it? If I'm pregnant, we're having a baby."

She could see he couldn't argue her point. Ready or not, if they were going to have a baby, then that was a huge responsibility. After running his fingers through his hair with a heavy exhale, he turned and left the bathroom with a curse.

She followed him into the kitchen. A yip told her Punzie had gotten up. She turned and crouched to lift the furry cutie. Her soft whimpers and cuddling face comforted Jaslene, especially when she saw Cal leaning over the sink as though he'd just lost everything he held dear. She sat on one of the tall chairs.

After a few minutes, Cal finally pushed off the sink and walked over to her. He leaned toward her with a hand on the table, looking at the now sleeping dog in Jaslene's lap and then up into Jaslene's eyes.

"Okay, fast-forward to when we have this baby," he said. "How do you envision your life?"

"You mean…with the baby?"

"With everything. Work. Me. The baby."

"Well, like you I haven't had time to think it over, but my first knee-jerk reaction is I'd take some time off work. As for you, I don't know. I suppose I'd be willing to live together to see if it works out."

He nodded a few times and she couldn't tell if he liked her answer. "What about my work?"

She began to sense he faced his biggest fears: losing another woman because of his line of work or because she was all wrong for him. Throw a baby into the mix and things got much more complicated.

"That's up to you, Cal." She reached up and put her

hand on his cheek. "No matter what happens between us, I won't keep you from seeing your child."

"So you think there's a chance you'd leave?"

How could she predict that? If the two of them got together and then it didn't work out, it wouldn't make any sense for them to stay together. "It wouldn't be your job that separated us, if that's what you need to know. I am not the kind of person who needs a man to be around every second."

He blinked once as though he was relieved to hear that.

Jaslene didn't say what thought came to her next— that she saw no reason why the two of them wouldn't be able to make a relationship work. They had chemistry but would that translate to romance and a family? How would a baby change that, though? They hadn't known each other very long, so what if their seemingly good match, personality-wise, changed?

"Let's make a doctor's appointment," he said. "I want to make sure you're all right, along with making sure you are, in fact, pregnant."

"I'll make one this morning." Did he mean to go with her? Jaslene didn't know how she felt about that. Good, in that he cared, but also wary. Dared she trust another man?

Later that day, Cal had to force himself to focus on Payton's case as he searched through her personal records for the second time since he'd begun the investigation. His tenacity—or the need for distraction—paid off. In a box containing operating manuals for various appliances, he found a receipt for the purchase of a disposable phone one month before she disappeared. Cal hadn't been the one to search this box and he could see how a receipt would be missed in a box full of operating manuals.

Where was the phone?

It wasn't in Payton's house. Hearing Jaslene talking to Payton's mother for her periodic updates on the case, he went to her in the kitchen and showed her the receipt. Jaslene saw it and her eyes widened with excitement.

"Hey, Pat, something just came up. Do you know if Payton had a disposable phone?" she asked and then listened. "All right. We will be right there."

"She said Payton keeps some memorabilia in *her closet*," Jaslene said.

Cal drove them to Patricia's house. Jaslene didn't say much on the way. He sensed she was not only glad for this significant lead, but for the distraction as well.

At Pat's house, it took them just moments to find a shoebox filled with things Payton had kept from her childhood. Among them, she had hidden the phone. Cal took that and the charger and he and Jaslene returned to her house. Cal plugged in the phone and stared at it, impatiently waiting for it to charge.

Jaslene held Rapunzel like a baby. That image didn't help the ever present worry of Jaslene being pregnant. He didn't need a doctor to tell him what lay ahead. Dread pooled and swirled in his guts. Yet, even as these negative feelings assaulted him in waves, so did the image of their baby growing inside of her, of the birth and of what would come after that. Less and less he thought of the risk to his heart and more of what the child would be like, and what it would be like to be a father, something he'd long ago abandoned all hope of experiencing.

She walked toward him and then turned, gently bouncing Rapunzel as though putting her to sleep. With her back presented to him, he once again had the sight of her rear in faded blue jeans. The front of her top scooped down and draped over her breasts and then flared attractively. He watched her until she turned again and saw him. Their eyes met for a few long seconds, heating the energy between them.

"Has it charged enough?" Jaslene asked.

Glad she'd redirected his attention, Cal checked and saw the cell had enough juice to start looking. He navigated through her phone calls, Jaslene leaning close to look with him.

"That's Dr. Benjamin's." When he came to a number he didn't recognize, she pointed. "What's that one?"

"Let's find out."

"Why did she have a burner phone?" she asked as he dialed the number to another detective at DAI.

"She didn't want anything traced to her." She was afraid of being discovered. Had she gotten the phone to communicate with the married doctor and hide her relationship with him? Cal didn't think so. She wasn't the one married. Dr. Benjamin was.

"Oscar," he said into his cell. A few seconds later Oscar, an expert in mobile device forensics, answered.

"You have something for me?" Oscar asked, sounding excited.

"Is it a slow day at DAI?" Cal chuckled.

"Slow week, which is a good thing because that means fewer people are being killed, but it makes for dull days for me."

"I have a number I need you to track down."

"Is that all? What about the phone it's on?"

"I'll send it to you overnight delivery."

"Yay."

Cal gave him the number.

"Hang on. I can locate that device for you right now."

Cal heard him typing into his high-tech computer program.

Then Oscar whistled. "West Virginia Insurance Fraud Unit. Was Payton reporting insurance fraud on her married doctor lover?"

"If she did, there would have been an investigation."

"Are you sure there wasn't?"

He hadn't checked, but wouldn't Dr. Benjamin be out of work if he committed insurance fraud? People went to jail for that.

"I think you have motive, friend. Maybe the married doctor had her whacked to stop her."

"Maybe. Depends on whether he was defrauding people. Thanks, Oscar."

"Send me that phone."

"It's on the way." He put down his phone and looked at Jaslene. "Time to investigate Dr. Benjamin's business."

"Why would Payton buy a disposable phone?" Jaslene asked.

"To hide her calls to the fraud unit."

"Yeah, but he had to have known the number. She used it to call him."

"She must have wanted the calls to be traceable but she didn't want him to know she was onto something."

"Why not use her own phone?"

"She could toss this one if she needed to."

She pondered that awhile, still seeming skeptical.

Payton must have known he might try to find the phone, either to see what calls she'd made on her second phone or to see if she'd called the fraud unit. "If he was suspicious of her, he'd want to know why she'd purchased a second phone." Her regular cell phone records had been searched long ago, with nothing suspicious turning up.

"Or if he found out she was onto him."

"Exactly. Tomorrow let's go talk to some people about the good doctor's business."

She nodded, looking somber. "Right after my appointment."

Stepping into the ob-gyn's office, Jaslene could feel Cal's tension. She had a fair amount of her own. Amazement gave her chills every once in a while. Anxiety had its turn as well. Over the last few days she'd had time to get used to the idea of having a baby, but not how to handle Cal. Even if they could come to terms with their past experiences in other relationships, the timing was all wrong. A baby? She reeled with incredulity. She chastised herself for losing track of her cycle.

That didn't mean Jaslene wasn't beginning to look

forward to having a child in her life. More and more the idea grew on her, expanded and took shape into a warm feeling. She wondered about names. Boy or girl? She wasn't sure which she'd prefer more.

"You've got a funny smile on your face."

Jaslene turned from the television screen in the waiting room. Cal looked wary and intent on finding out why.

She shrugged. "I was just thinking." She turned away again.

"About what?"

Forced to address him, she opened her mouth to say *the baby* when a nurse called, "Jaslene?"

Her heart lurched and she had to breathe deeper. She stared at the nurse without moving. This would confirm what she and Cal already knew but needed to make official.

Cal stood and extended his hand. Startled, she took his and he guided her to stand with him. He didn't let go as he walked toward the waiting nurse. That surprised her. He was so upset over this, and yet he'd stepped up to the plate like a brave, confident player. Ready to take them in for a home run.

The nurse led them down a hall and directed Jaslene into a bathroom, where she provided a urine sample. Cal waited outside the door and so did the nurse.

"Right this way." The nurse took them to a room and asked Jaslene a set of routine questions, took her vitals, drew some blood and then said, "The doctor will be in shortly."

Once she left, Jaslene perched on the exam table

while Cal sat on a chair, wringing his hands, leaning over with his head down.

He really didn't want this. Was it disenchantment caused by his first marriage? Did he not trust Jaslene? Or did he not believe they'd make a good family? He'd already said he wasn't ready for a baby. Neither was she, but she wouldn't drag him down.

"We'll be fine, Cal." When he looked up at her, she said, "Me and the baby. You don't have to do anything you aren't comfortable with. Women raise kids on their own all the time these days. I have a good job. I can take care of the baby on my own."

The anger she'd seen in him before began to re-appear, his eyes going hard and his jaw clenching. "You're suggesting I forget I have a child?"

Jaslene had nothing to say to that. She would never be able to forget her own child and gave him credit for not being able to do so, either. They were both stuck with this.

The door opened with a knock and Jaslene's doctor entered. In a white jacket, she had dark, short, curly hair and soft hazel eyes.

"Hello, Jaslene."

"Hello."

"This must be your significant other?"

"Calum Chelsey." He shook the doctor's hand, half rising off the chair.

She smiled kindly and went to her chair and the computer. "Just here for the pregnancy test?" She began typing away.

"Yes."

"Well, if you're here, I'm sure it will come as no shock that the test confirmed you are pregnant." The doctor finished typing and turned to face her, looking at Cal, too. "Was this planned?"

Jaslene scoffed. "No."

"How long have the two of you been together?"

Jaslene glanced at Cal, who also looked her way.

"Not long," Cal said.

"Love crept up on you, hmm?" The doctor smiled. "It happens. You aren't alone. The question is what you want to do."

"We're having the baby." Jaslene noticed how Cal glanced at her when she said *we.*

"That's good. We'll set up regular checkups and get you on a healthy diet with some supplements and exercise. There's also a Lamaze class I can recommend." She looked at Cal and then put her hand on Jaslene's knee. "You may even start to like this. I know you'll develop a bond with the baby. And if you aren't sure about the relationship the two of you share together, this might be the thing to get you closer. Babies can work magic."

"Thank you, Doctor. It has been quite a surprise." She felt how little that conveyed just how disruptive this was to her—and to Cal. The baby was blameless, though, an innocent life created by two people who should have known better.

"I'm here for you whenever you need me. And if you want to see a counselor, I can recommend someone for that as well."

Cal's body language was rigid and full of tension. The thoughts that must be going through his head! He was going to be a father. He didn't know the mother of his child well enough. Although they'd known each other quite a while professionally, they hadn't known each other long enough as lovers…or parents.

Having the phone as a new lead in Payton's case helped take Jaslene's mind off the looming reality that they'd confirmed her pregnancy. Their first stop after her doctor's appointment was to see Bonita Lawrence. They intercepted her when she arrived home at her apartment and invited her for some coffee.

Jaslene sat beside Cal at a booth in a downtown Chesterville coffee shop. Booths lined the windows and round wood tables filled the space between there and the kitchen and bathrooms. Historic town pictures covered the walls. About half the tables were occupied. Jaslene had ordered herbal tea and Cal and Bonita got coffees.

"What did you want to talk to me about?" Bonita asked.

Cal said, "We'd like to understand more about Dr. Benjamin's business practices. Can you help us with that?"

He didn't reveal Payton had called the fraud unit. Surely he didn't want word getting around to Benjamin too soon.

"I don't know. Depends on what you want to know." She sipped her latte.

"He's got his regular practice, but he also has other clinics. What do they do?"

"He's got two surgical offices, two family practices and the home health care offices."

"How does that work? Do the doctors rent space from him?"

She shook her head. "No. They all work for him."

"Have you ever noticed him diagnosing anyone with something they didn't need or anything that seemed unusual?"

"No."

"How is the insurance handled in all the offices? Do they manage their own or does he have a department dedicated to that?"

"I didn't work with the insurance at all, but I do know he had a referral program where doctors who referred patients to his offices received a bonus of some sort. It's how he grew his business to what it is today."

That made sense. The more doctors referring to his practice, the more patients he had and the more money he made. But that couldn't be the only way he'd grown his practice.

"Did he have any other incentive programs?" she asked.

"Not that I know of."

"What about any other business policies?" Cal added, "Anything relating to a patient's treatment?"

"As much as I don't like him, I have to say he was very thorough. He has high ratings. Patients love him."

Some a little too much, perhaps. Payton, for example.

"Do you know of anyone we can talk to in the home health care offices?" Cal asked.

Jaslene didn't think they'd get much more from this woman, either.

"Yeah. I have a friend who's a nurse at one of them. I can give you her name."

Cal wondered about Bonita's comment on how thorough Dr. Benjamin was with his patients. From an insurance angle, maybe he'd been too thorough. The referral program didn't seem unusual, just good business sense.

Jaslene reached the town house door ahead of him. Sandy Pennington, the nurse Bonita told them about, lived here. Bonita had even phoned her friend for them, so she was expecting them.

He could still smell the body spray Jaslene used. It was subtle and he'd begun to identify her by smell alone. Still in the faded blue jeans and flaring gray sweater, she'd drawn his gaze more than once since leaving the doctor's office and finding out they were going to be parents.

Sandy opened the door with a wary smile. "Hi. You must be the detectives."

Cal didn't correct her. "Thanks for agreeing to talk to us."

"Come in." She stepped aside. "It's getting cold outside."

Cal let Jaslene inside ahead of him, closing the door in a small entry.

"Bonita said you wanted to know about Dr. Benjamin's home health care divisions?" Sandy sat on the sectional.

Jaslene sat adjacent from her, so Cal did the same.

"We wondered if you could tell us how the home health care is run and who handles the insurance," Cal said.

"Insurance." She seemed curious why he'd ask such a thing. "Well, we're assigned patients and make our rounds. We have paperwork we complete for the insurance and turn that in to administration. They file all the claims."

"Are you ever instructed to do work that isn't necessary?"

"Not that I've noticed. The patients' care is our top priority. Most of them feel well taken care of. That's one of the reasons I love working where I do."

"Do you ever work with Dr. Benjamin?" Jaslene asked.

"No, but Bonita told me plenty. I feel bad for her but I have a good job and I don't have to deal with him."

Cal noticed Jaslene scratch her ear and then fidget with her hands in her lap. Was she suspicious over how everyone had such nice things to say about the doctor? He was.

Chapter 13

Jaslene agreed with Cal that they shouldn't talk to Dr. Benjamin about Payton's call to the fraud unit. If he knew they were onto him—really onto him—and if he had something to do with Payton's disappearance, there was no telling what he'd do. Returning from Sandy's, they entered her house to hear Rapunzel yipping. Potty trained, she had the run of the house. Why was she not rushing to greet them? Apprehension reared up.

Cal held his arm out, an indication for her to stop.

The sudden sound of footfalls in the living room preceded the appearance of Riley. Jaslene sucked in a frightened breath. Armed with a gun, he fired as he ran past the laundry room. Cal shoved Jaslene behind the cover of the closet, grunting as though he'd been hit.

She didn't have time to check. He drew his pistol and ran after Riley.

Carefully, she followed. In the area between the kitchen and living room, she saw Cal chase after Riley through the back door. She also saw blood on his arm.

"Cal!" He had been hit! She rushed to the door but he was already sprinting across the backyard after Riley.

To her horror, Riley reached the fence and turned his gun on Cal. But Cal ducked behind the grill in time and fired back as Riley climbed over the fence and cried out, indicating Cal had struck his target.

Running to the fence, Cal jumped high and catapulted over. He must not be seriously injured if he could still do that.

Jaslene reached for the phone and dialed 911 as Rapunzel appeared in the kitchen, barking urgently. She ran into the living room, stopping to look back at her owner. When Jaslene didn't move, she barked and returned to the kitchen before running again into the living room.

"Nine-one-one, what's your emergency?"

Jaslene followed the puppy, who'd grown in the last several weeks. "Someone broke into my house."

The operator asked if the address she had was correct as Rapunzel trotted down the hall to the master bedroom.

"Yes, that's correct."

Rapunzel barked at the bed.

"Where is the intruder now?"

"He ran away."

Seeing nothing out of place, Jaslene crouched and looked underneath and saw what looked like a bomb.

"Oh my God. There is a bomb in my house!" Dropping the phone, she picked up the puppy and ran from the bedroom, through the house to the front door. Outside, she ran to the sidewalk and searched for Cal. She doubted he'd climb back over the fence. Hearing more gunfire, she worried he'd been hit again, especially when she spotted a motorcycle speeding around the corner down the block. She ran to the yard next door and took cover behind a tree.

Holding Rapunzel close, she waited for an explosion as the motorcycle neared. Her house could explode and Riley could shoot her. He still had a gun and aimed it at her. She cringed behind the tree as bark flew. Rapunzel whimpered and squirmed.

Gunfire from down the street told her Cal wasn't far. As the motorcycle sped away, the shooting stopped.

Cal ran to them and breathlessly watched Riley get away. Sirens grew louder.

"Why are you outside?" Cal asked.

"There's a bomb under my bed."

His breathing faltered in alarm. "What?"

Emergency vehicles arrived, along with a bomb squad. Jaslene waited anxiously to find out if her house would explode.

Cal did not like the fact that Riley had gotten away from him—again. He had nearly destroyed Jaslene's house and partially burned his down. The bomb squad had disarmed the bomb in time, luckily.

"Why does he keep trying to kill us?" Jaslene asked.

They sat on the sofa in the living room with a documentary playing, Rapunzel curled in a furry ball on one end next to Jaslene.

Riley had fake-shot a gun at them first, fired at them when they'd found him in hiding, then he'd broken into both of their homes and set Cal's house on fire, but one thing stood out to Cal. The man who'd driven by shooting had worn a mask. The person who had started the fire had also worn a mask. Had that also been Riley or had it been someone else?

The bullet shell casings from all the scenes matched, except for those found at the drive-by. Riley could have more than one gun, but what if someone else was also trying to kill them? The masked man in the drive-by seemed to have been be more professional than Riley. He'd only try to kill them if he had a solid opportunity. The drive-by had the advantage of surprise and a short period of time. Also, the masked man hid his identity. Riley had not, almost as though he'd wanted them to know who was after them.

"Revenge is making him brazen," he said.

"He was obsessed with Payton before she disappeared. Killing me because he blames me makes no sense."

"It does if he didn't kill her. He was forced to stay away from her, then she went missing. Remember? According to Riley, she'd still be here if she hadn't broken things off with him."

Jaslene gave him a closer look. "How is it not Riley? We've seen him."

"Remember the drive-by? The fire?"

"Almost every time I close my eyes."

"The driver wore a mask."

She took a few seconds to ponder that. "We need to find out if Dr. Benjamin is involved in insurance fraud. That could point us to the real culprit."

"My thoughts exactly. Rapunzel isn't the only detective in the making."

Just then Jaslene's cell rang. She reached over Rapunzel to get her phone and answered.

Cal saw her face turn down into a concerned frown. "What's wrong?"

Jaslene stood and so did Cal.

"When did they come by?"

Jaslene covered her mouth with her hand and stared at Cal as she listened to a long dialogue on the other end. She closed her eyes a few times and her eyes began to tear up.

"Was she drowned?" Jaslene wiped her eye and breathed to control her emotions.

Right then Cal knew Payton's body had been discovered.

"Strangled?" Jaslene asked.

Strangled in her house and then dumped or strangled somewhere else? Questions fired away in his head.

Jaslene looked at Cal again. "They think someone put her in the river?"

Strangled, then dumped.

"Do they have any ideas on who might have done it?" he asked.

"They're questioning people in the area now," she said to Cal, and then she told the caller, "If you need help planning services, I'm here for you, okay?"

Jaslene listened for a brief time longer and then said a somber goodbye. She stared down at the phone awhile. "Payton's body was found on the bank of a river earlier today. That was her mother. Her parents have just identified the body. She called to let me know because I was her closest friend."

Tears dripped down her cheeks, springing free on what had to be a big wave of sorrow.

"Oh, baby." He went to her and took her into his arms. "I'm so sorry."

She sobbed softly against him a few moments. Cal took her phone and set it on the coffee table. She gripped his shirt at his back when he embraced her firmly again. He rubbed her back.

"I know you hurt but you must have known it could come to this," he said as gently as he could.

She nodded against his shoulder, followed by a sniffle and more sobs.

"Her body will lead us to her killer, Jaslene. I won't let him get away with this. I promise." He rubbed her back some more. "Take comfort in that."

She leaned back, eyes reddened and face wet. His heart lurched with the need to make her feel better. If he could take her sadness into him he would, to spare her this pain.

All he could do was bend a little and kiss her, not hard, just a soft, reassuring kiss to let her know he was here for her.

Her breathing was unsteady and she sniffled. He leaned back in search of a tissue. There was a box on the side table.

Rapunzel sat up and watched with round, innocent eyes.

Cal gave Jaslene a few tissues. Her crying had eased, but he slid his arms loosely around her. She blew her nose and gracefully dropped the wad onto the coffee table.

"I have to go to work now," he said. "I need to talk to the detectives who processed her body." He'd also get on them about not calling him. He should have been on the scene.

"Can I go with you?" she asked, taking another tissue and dabbing her eyes.

"I'm going to the coroner's. I'd rather you go stay with a friend. I'll drop you off and pick you up when I'm done. I'll fill you in on everything after."

When she still didn't agree, he said, "I don't want you to see her body, Jaslene, and I need to know you're somewhere safe."

At last she nodded, clearly not wanting to see her friend's body. "I'll call Tatum. Catherine will probably join us when she finds out."

"Give me the address. I'll get another detective to watch over you. Let me make some calls. You go and get ready to go."

"Wait."

Jaslene stopped from opening the car door to get out. Cal had just stopped in front of Tatum's house.

She watched him walk around the front of his SUV and then open her door. He must be pampering her because she was so upset.

She got out and stood before him on the sidewalk. "Thanks."

He slid his arm around her and brought her close. Looking into her eyes, magnetizing her with warmth, he touched her chin with two fingers and kissed her.

The touch of his lips made her shiver with desire.

"Good luck in there," he said with affection in his eyes. Then he looked into the street.

She glanced back and saw a car parked behind Cal's SUV. That must be the other detective.

Cal kissed her again.

She wasn't looking forward to telling her friends about Payton. She'd told Tatum she'd be stopping by and to call Catherine, who'd probably already guessed Jaslene had news to share.

"See you soon." She moved away from his embrace and the smile that came to her wasn't forced. He had made her feel good when she was so heartbroken over Payton.

He grinned back and then winked.

Obviously he'd forgotten she was pregnant. Or maybe he was adjusting to the idea.

Turning, she headed for the three-paneled glass and brown-framed front door of Tatum's house.

Catherine stood in the hardwood entry with her arms folded over a football sweatshirt. She wore faded jeans and tennis shoes.

"What was that all about?" Tatum asked.

"The last time we talked you didn't seem very fond of your detective. You look more than fond now," Catherine said.

Jaslene closed the front door behind her and moved farther into the entry without answering.

She had bad news to tell them first. "I asked to meet you here because something happened."

"Come on in." Tatum led them into the great room.

Jaslene sat on the pink sofa next to Catherine, and Tatum took one of the chairs. She'd put out a pitcher of iced herbal tea on the big square coffee table with a white vase of green hydrangeas and a stack of books. Jaslene poured herself a glass and Catherine took the next glass. Tatum didn't move to do the same.

Jaslene held the glass, struggling with a way to come out and say their good friend was confirmed dead.

"What's the matter, Jaslene?" Tatum asked. "You sounded so urgent on the phone."

"They found her body, didn't they?" Catherine said. She'd never been one to gloss anything over, so Jaslene shouldn't be surprised she'd blurted that out.

"She was strangled and her body was dumped in the Elk River." Jaslene stood and walked to the window, rubbing her arm. "Her mother called me not long ago and told me. She identified the body."

"Her body was still intact?" Catherine asked, standing and coming to Jaslene, who faced her.

"Catherine," Tatum admonished, standing as well.

"What? It's been a long time since she died."

"Listening to you, people would think you didn't even know Payton."

Catherine cocked her head in protest.

All this talk of Payton as a body bothered Jaslene. She remembered her long red hair, green eyes and unique style of dressing and couldn't bring herself to picture her rotting in a river.

"I don't know any details yet," she said after a swallow, "but her body must have been preserved somehow." Or she had been held captive and killed recently. Jaslene shuddered with the thought.

"My last memory of her is when we all went shopping and caught a movie. Remember that day?" Tatum's eyes grew bittersweet.

That was a good day. Payton had been so animated, cracking jokes and talking about her newest story. Jaslene had seen her once more after that and also talked to her on the phone. But nothing had cued her that something was wrong or Payton had any reason to fear for her life.

"We went to her house after that and drank wine and talked until two in the morning," Catherine said, having sobered. "She talked about going to Europe together."

"We were going to plan the trip at our next lunch," Tatum said.

Jaslene remembered how excited she was with the idea. She wiped a tear from beneath her eye and then another, sniffling.

"I'm sorry, Jaslene," Catherine said, starting to cry with her. "I never believed we'd find her alive."

Tatum hugged her and cried, too, Catherine making it a three-person hug. They cried for a while and then gradually eased out of the embrace.

Tatum grabbed a tissue box from the bathroom and they all blew their noses.

"When will you know more?" Tatum asked.

"As soon as Cal picks me up. He's going to the coroner's office now."

"Cal…" Tatum said in a leading tone. "Why don't you tell us what's going on between you? We could use some happier news right now."

"He kissed you," Catherine said. "Are you finally getting over Ryan?"

"That was a nice kiss, too," Tatum said with a sniffle but she had to tell them something.

"We sort of…started…you know."

"You slept together?" Catherine said, looking thrilled.

"Who needs to ask that?" Tatum said. "Didn't you see the way he kissed her?"

"There's more," Jaslene said. She might as well get this over with. Once she had her friends' rapt attention, she said, "I'm pregnant."

Both women made sounds of excitement. Catherine let out a long, "Ooh!" Tatum shrieked and went to her, bending down for a hug.

"That's so wonderful!"

"I hoped you'd have children with Ryan," Catherine said. "I'm so happy for you."

"When is the wedding?" Tatum asked.

"Uh…" Jaslene went back to the sofa and sat. "We didn't exactly plan on this."

"Of course you didn't but from the looks of it, you two are meant for each other anyway." Tatum went to a chair and sat. Catherine took the other chair.

They did have chemistry but that wasn't enough to last a lifetime with someone…or was there something more between them?

"You don't seem sure." Catherine examined her face.

"I'm not, really."

"Do you still feel guilty about that guy who kissed you before Ryan died?"

Jaslene was struck suddenly with the realization that she didn't. Baffled, she had to take a few seconds to gather herself. She hadn't even thought about Ryan since having sex with Cal. Why? The answer slammed her almost instantly. Being with Cal felt right when she wasn't analyzing all the reasons why they might not work.

"It took you two years to get over that," Catherine said.

"No, to find the right *man*," Tatum interjected.

Tatum might have a point. Maybe it had taken a man who made her feel the way Ansel had. Except Cal made her feel much more than Ansel, which gave her a flash of a different kind of guilt over her marriage with Ryan. Had she not loved him at all?

"We don't mean to make you feel bad, Jaslene, especially now, with the news about Payton."

Jaslene looked at Tatum. "I don't. I just realized I never knew what love was until…" She stopped.

Love?

"I mean, Ryan and I were close, but we were friends. We respected each other and enjoyed each other's company, but we didn't have that spark."

Catherine and Tatum stared at her.

"I don't love Cal," Jaslene said.

They continued to stare, Catherine taking a drink of her iced tea and eyeing her dubiously. And maybe with a little envy? Jaslene wondered.

Cal had to wait for the coroner, but finally the medium-height man with eerie blue eyes sunk into their sockets appeared with an equally strange smile. He'd always thought coroners would have to be a bit of the odd sort to do what they did.

"Detective Chelsey." His voice boomed with friend-liness.

Cal shook Dr. Kenney's hand. If ever there was a case where a man's look contrasted with his personality, this was it.

"I heard you left the department."

"Yes. I went private."

"I heard that, too. I've worked with another former detective from your agency before. Quite an impressive group you are."

"Thanks. I'm hoping you've got something impressive for me today."

"Yes, yes. Come with me."

Cal walked beside the long-striding expert in pathology down a hall toward two metal doors.

"The body was mildly decomposed, preserved enough in the neck and head area to determine the cause of death." The doctor pushed open a door and Cal the other.

The open room looked sterile beneath blinding bright lights, metal and white tile grabbing the eye first, particularly the embalming tables. Shelves packed with supplies ran the far wall, and a counter with drawers must have contained all the sharp objects.

"She was put inside a plastic wrapping, like the kind you see at construction sites." The doctor pulled out a refrigerated drawer to reveal a body inside a white cloth. "Her killer must have dumped her in a deep part of the river where the temperature stayed relatively consistent." He pulled back the cloth.

Cal had seen many dead bodies but had difficulty every time. This body had once been a lively, beautiful woman with a productive life and a future that should have never been taken from her. The discolored, bony object on the rollout table resembled nothing of that person. She had become evidence. In death, she'd help him catch her killer by speaking from the grave, as it were.

He noticed the markings still partially visible on her deteriorating neck.

"There were rope fibers embedded in what's left of her skin," the doctor said. "They're being examined by Forensics, but I think they'll match the rope tied to her ankles and a cement block." Reaching over to a counter, he picked up a report and handed it to him. "That's your copy."

Cal's detective contacts must have arranged for this. He skimmed through the sections. "He strangled her with the rope he used to sink her body?"

"That's my assessment."

It was a good one.

"Was she murdered at the river?"

"Definitely not. The lividity is more prominent on her rear and back than what I found on her right side."

The body had been moved. Payton had been lying on her back after she died and then placed onto her right side afterward. How had the killer managed to strangle her and transport her to the river? Had she met him at the park where Payton's car had been found? Cal doubted she'd gone there herself. She was either forced or taken there after she was killed.

Murdering someone in a public park would be risky. Payton had likely been murdered at her home. For that to occur, the killer would have had to drive her car to the park, which meant there had to have been another vehicle waiting. The killer could have left his vehicle and walked to Payton's house to kill her. She didn't live far from there.

"She floated to the surface when her feet separated from the rope. This can happen during decomposition."

The crime scene detectives must have found the block and rope. "How do you know the rope was attached to her feet?"

"There were fragments still around a portion of

one of her ankles." The doctor showed him the area of Payton's ankles, or what was left of one of them. "Forensics has all the evidence. You'll get a copy of the report."

"Good. I've seen enough. Thank you, Doctor."

"I'd say it was my pleasure. Unfortunately, I am not the bearer of good news."

"In my case it is. I have a body. Now I can catch the killer and put him away for life."

"I appreciate the optimism. I'll show you out."

Cal left the coroner's office and decided to drive the distance between the park and Payton's house. He reminded himself that police records said no one saw another car in the parking lot at that time. Payton's car had been left there between 8:00 and 10:00 p.m., based on her estimated time of death.

At the park, he sat in his vehicle and studied the surroundings. Someone walked their dog along the sidewalk. Two moms watched from a bench as their kids played in the playground.

Across the street three houses had a good view of the park. Cal got out of his SUV and walked to the sidewalk. He searched all around him, checking out the houses farther down from the park.

As he neared the corner of Payton's street, he reached a house with a security sign. Stopping when he spotted motion detectors, he looked for cameras. There was one on the front porch. Walking back up the sidewalk, he turned and walked the same path, this time watching the camera. A tiny red light came on as he passed.

Cal walked up the driveway to the porch and rang the bell. A dog barked and then he heard a woman say, "No."

The door opened a crack to reveal a green-eyed, short-haired blonde in a white sweater and jeans. He could smell her perfume already. Cal opened his wallet to show her his identification, stating he was a private investigator with Dark Alley Investigations.

"My name is Calum Chelsey. I'm a private detective investigating a murder. May I ask you some questions?"

"Me?"

"Payton Everett went missing seven months ago from the park up the street. We think the killer may have walked by your house the night she disappeared." He looked up at the camera. "I saw that you have surveillance."

The door opened wider and the woman looked from the camera to him. "Seven months ago is a long time. I don't know if my husband keeps the recordings that long."

"May I have a look?"

"It would be better if you came back when he's home."

"Of course. When will that be?"

"He usually comes home from work by about five thirty."

"Thanks. I'll come back then."

Cal left the porch and walked back toward his SUV. If he was right and the killer parked his car before walking to Payton's house to murder her, the security surveillance would be a huge break in the case. He needed some luck. He hoped like hell those residents hadn't deleted any recordings.

Chapter 14

Cal arrived back at Tatum's house. The moment he stepped out of his SUV, he knew something was wrong. The front door was open and he heard screaming. He looked for the man he had asked to watch over Jaslene and saw that Detective Kennedy was not in his car.

Drawing his gun, he ran to the door and cautiously entered. Tatum and Catherine stood huddled with Jaslene in front of the fireplace as a masked man aimed a gun at them. His back was to Cal. He must have just surprised them.

Jaslene looked terrified. Cal forced himself to remain calm. If anything happened to her, he would be so angry.

In the kitchen the detective watching the house was lying on the floor, blood pooling beneath him.

Tatum saw Cal and he hoped the shift of her eyes hadn't given away his presence. Jaslene might have seen him but she didn't reveal so. The masked man blocked Catherine's view.

"You're coming with me," the man said to Jaslene.

Cal approached in stealthy silence. Reaching the man's back, he pressed his gun to the side of his head.

"Drop it or I'll splatter your brains," he told the masked man.

The villain froze and slowly lifted his hands, the gun still in one hand.

The women dispersed, Tatum and Catherine rushing around the man and into the kitchen, where Cal hoped they would help Detective Kennedy. Jaslene took the pistol from the masked man.

"Turn around," Cal told the man.

He did, slowly. He was a big man, the same height as Cal. Jaslene scurried farther away, joining Tatum and Catherine. He heard Tatum calling 911.

Cal reached up and pulled the mask off, ruffling his thick, wavy black hair. The man's dark eyes pinned him with emotionless patience. Cal didn't recognize him but he could see he was a professional. The way he stood there unfazed, as though waiting for an opportunity, told him as much.

Cal stepped back and out of reach. "Who sent you here?"

The man didn't respond.

"Who is paying you?" Cal demanded.

"He was going to take Jaslene," Catherine had appeared from around the corner, sounding as though she'd caught her breath from the fright she and the other women had just gone through.

"What then?" Cal asked the man. "Were you hoping to lure me and kill us both?"

The man remained silent.

"We all know you didn't come here for a social visit. None of these women invited you. Who hired you?" Cal didn't expect an answer. "Riley Sawyer?"

The man continued to meet his eyes.

"Dr. Benjamin?"

"He didn't tell me his name," the man said.

Progress. "Oh, then how did he find you?"

"I don't know. He called me one day and asked me to meet him. I did."

"And agreed to what?"

The man didn't answer.

"How much is he paying you?"

Nothing.

"Come on. I've got enough right now to put you away. You were armed and you're an intruder. You were going to kidnap Jaslene. Those are some serious charges."

"You aren't a cop." He lowered his hands shoulder height.

So he'd been told enough about him and Jaslene to know Cal wasn't a detective any longer. "I don't have to be. Look, you can make this a lot easier on yourself if you talk. Do you really want to protect someone you don't even know? You're going to jail. For how long depends on how cooperative you are. What did he want you to do?"

The man seemed to waver. "He wants you and the girl dead."

"And you're the man he hired to do that?"

"I didn't say that."

If Riley wanted revenge, he might have hired this man to bring Cal and Jaslene somewhere where he could dole out his form of justice. The only problem with that theory was that Riley apparently didn't care whether anyone knew it was him who came after Cal and Jaslene. The person who hired this man cared about not being identified. Why would Riley hire someone when he'd already been seen trying to kill them? Besides, Riley wasn't wealthy. Benjamin was.

"What's your name?" Cal asked.

The man moved his hands lightning fast and produced a knife from his waist. Cal blocked his attempt to swing and kicked the man backward.

He had his aim restored as the man stumbled. Jaslene appeared from the kitchen, still holding the gun.

The man regained his balance as Catherine screeched and tried to veer out of the way. The man grabbed her to use as a shield.

No way was another bad guy getting away from him. He was sick of them getting the better of him. And he would stop at nothing to protect the women, especially Jaslene…and their unborn child.

"Don't do it," Cal ordered. "I will shoot."

The man started to haul Catherine so she'd be backed up against him.

Cal fired before he could, putting a hole in the man's shoulder. He yelped, dropped the knife and went down.

Going to the man, he kicked the knife away and kept his gun trained on his head. "Move. Give me an excuse."

The man held his hands out. Cal crouched and patted his body and found another pistol in his boot. Tossing that where the knife lay, he straightened. The man held his shoulder, grimacing.

Sirens grew louder outside. He looked up to see Jaslene with one arm around Catherine, aiming the pistol at the man, looking brave. He was so proud of her.

Cal went to her and touched her face with his palm. "Are you all right?"

"Yes."

He looked to Catherine. "How about you?"

"I'm okay. Really glad you showed up when you did."

"Keep the gun on him." Cal rushed into the kitchen, where Tatum knelt beside Detective Kennedy, pressing a cloth to his shoulder. He had begun to regain consciousness. Cal saw that he must have hit his head on the table as he fell.

The police and paramedics arrived. Cal got out of the way so the paramedics could work on Kennedy.

Then, seeing police had control of the would-be abductor, he went to Jaslene and took her into his arms.

All Jaslene wanted to do was go home, take a bath and cuddle with Rapunzel, but Cal told her about the security camera and she had to keep going for a little while longer. She couldn't believe how close she had come to being kidnapped. And probably killed.

It wasn't only her she had to protect. She had a baby, too. That thought alone had been the most terrifying during her ordeal. It had also been the thing that made her pick up the gun. She would have shot that masked man if she had to.

Right now she stood beside him at the door of the house where he'd stopped earlier. A man with a brown, neatly trimmed mustache answered.

"Detective Chelsey?"

"Yes."

"My wife told me you stopped by." He opened the door to allow them inside. "I'm not sure I'll be any help but you're welcome to take a look at the photos on file."

He kept them? Maybe they'd run into some luck tonight. Excitement perked her up. This was getting exhausting.

He led them through the house and into an office.

The man stood aside at the desk where a computer screen displayed a file folder.

"My wife told me the missing woman you're looking for is Payton Everett. She lives around the corner from us. I opened the files for the day she went missing. Nothing stood out to me but maybe you'll see something I didn't."

Cal sat at the computer and began opening files. Jaslene remained standing to his right and watched him go through the files. A courier had delivered a package that day and two people walking their dogs passed by. A man passed by.

"Can I make copies of these?" Cal asked.

"Of course."

He took a flash drive from his front shirt pocket, having put it there hoping he'd be able to use it. After saving the file, he viewed the open one closer, magnifying it.

"It's hard to see his face," Jaslene said.

The man was too tall to be Riley and wore a hoodie and jeans. She could think of only one other man this could be, but they would both need proof.

Once they arrived home, Jaslene went into the tub, where Cal had lit some candles for her. He'd pampered her ever since he'd rescued her and her friends from that awful man. Riley was still on the loose. Police were still searching for him. Sinking into the sudsy water, she relaxed back. A knock on the door turned her head. She'd left the door open, maybe because she didn't want to be alone right now.

Cal entered. "Is it okay if I sit in here?"

"Yes."

He sat on the edge of the tub. "You sure you're all right? All that stress can't be good on you."

"I'm fine. A bath and a good night's sleep is all I need. And maybe Rapunzel." She smiled, silently adding, *And you by my side*.

"You gave me a big scare today," he said.

"I was scared, too."

"No, I mean, I thought of what would have happened if you'd have been hurt. Or worse?"

He'd been torn up over that. Was that the detective in him or something more personal? Probably a little of both but she fancied he'd been torn up for personal reasons more than professional.

"I'm all right."

He stood then and began to undress. She knew he intended to join her and she didn't stop him. Even while her protective instincts warned to, she didn't. Something deeper welcomed his company. It was due to the ordeal today, yes, but also more than that.

He slipped into the water opposite her. "I don't want you out of my sight anymore."

She moved her legs to make room for him, her knees poking out of the sudsy water. "We're going to bathe together now?" He must need the closeness as much as she did.

"Tonight we are."

She rested her calves on his right thigh and grew more curious as to why he needed to be close. She met his gaze as he reclined in the water, just looking at her.

"Why does it bother you so much that I could have been hurt?" she asked, wanting to know if he would admit his feelings for her. "As opposed to anyone else."

"You're pregnant with our child, for one."

He seemed reluctant to go on to a second reason.

"For another…you must know I care about you. Do you really have to ask?"

She angled her head and sent him a look he couldn't mistake.

He glanced down and swished the water with this hands. Then he raised his eyes, his gaze sexy and intense.

"I keep thinking, what if I'd have been any later?" he finally said.

"Did that change the way you feel about the baby? About us?"

After several agonizing moments, he nodded twice. "I want the baby."

What about her?

"I don't know what to do with that," he said. "I also don't know what to do with how I feel about you."

"How do you feel about me?" she asked quietly, feeling her heart gush with love because he was opening up to her.

"Like I did when I met my first wife, only different. More."

Different. More. Her heart and soul soared as she rejoiced but only for a moment. He'd just said he didn't know what to do with how he felt after all.

"I used to imagine my wife pregnant," Cal said. "It was the best feeling in the world. Now, with you. I can't do that again."

He couldn't let himself feel that again. He distrusted. He resisted. He was afraid. Calum Chelsey, hotshot former detective who feared nothing, feared marriage and babies. Family.

"You don't have to imagine me pregnant. I *am* pregnant." Maybe that was part of what was different: their future wasn't conditional. It was a reality.

"Yes, and if my timing hadn't been so spot-on today, I could have lost you and the baby. It would have been much worse than losing my wife because I'd never know what it was like to give us a try, to be a family."

"Are you saying that's what you want to do now?"

"I think so. More than I did before I had a taste of what it would do to me if I lost you and the baby."

She rose up from her sitting position and crawled over to him, putting her hands on his manly shoulders and straddling him. Air cooled her wet skin and suds ran down her front, some sticking to her breasts. He loosely wrapped his arms around her, his eyes ravenously taking in her upper torso.

"It's hard for me, too." She ran her fingers down his damp chest. "I realized today that I no longer carry guilt over what happened with Ansel before my husband died. I've moved on and it's because of you."

Cal tipped his head back a little in question or doubt.

"I'm not saying I've fallen in love with you. I just think we fit, and for now, for starters, I think it's enough to move forward with what we've been handed."

"A baby."

She smiled, letting the intimate moment take her. "Yes."

The enormity of their situation hung between them, the way it had when they'd first realized she might be pregnant. Except this time it didn't come with the same punch.

Jaslene didn't know what tomorrow or the weeks ahead would bring. She would only make the best of it. And right now, the best was being with Cal, in the tub, in this moment.

Sliding her hands up his chest, she wrapped her arms around his neck, bringing her face close to his. "I think you'll make a great dad."

His eyes began to smolder and at first she thought

her compliment had the effect, but then she realized her breasts were pressed against his chest. Maybe the progress they'd made coming to terms with the baby made her warm to him, maybe their mutual need for company had. Maybe both. Neither stopped her from kissing him passionately.

He ran his hands up her back, bringing suds with them. Shivers spread over her water-cooled skin. When he held her head and deepened the kiss, the shivers became an internal combustion, and she moved against him desperately, feeling his hardness.

He withdrew from the kiss and cupped water in his hands, letting it run down her breasts, then repeated the process for her chilled arms. With her breasts now clear of bubbles, he took them one at a time into his mouth. She dug her fingers into his hair and closed her eyes to exquisite sensation.

When he'd satisfied himself with her chest, he kissed her shoulder leisurely made his way up her neck and back to her mouth. He turned Jaslene's insides into pure molten heat.

Unable to wait any longer, she rose up and found him, guiding him inside her.

He held her rear as she began to move, slow at first. Soon, he moved his hips from beneath her, just enough to find her sweet spot. She moved faster, going with the rising ecstasy that only he seemed capable of generating in her.

As she ground against him harder, water sloshed but she didn't care. All that mattered was Cal and what he did to her. She didn't stifle the sounds emitting from her throat that accompanied her sudden release and heard him join her in perfect synchrony.

As their bodies cooled, he kissed her gently a few times. The aftermath engulfed her and probably him the same way.

"You'll make a good mother, too," he said against her mouth.

She smiled against his lips and laughed huskily. She'd decided not thinking about tomorrow or the weeks ahead was the best thing for her. She might not feel the same way tomorrow, but she'd take today.

Chapter 15

The next day, Cal waited with Jaslene in Dr. Benjamin's office. They hadn't let on what they'd discovered and also shared with police, but it was time to make the doctor sweat. After finding the disposable phone, Cal was more certain than ever that Dr. Benjamin was behind the masked shooter, and Riley was an entirely different matter.

Their backs to the corner window, he watched the electronic photo frame go through picture after picture of his wife and kids. Jaslene idly glanced at the photos of sailboats on the walls and then joined him in observing the photo frame.

Then their gazes met. She smiled affectionately, eliciting a grin from him. Since their talk yesterday they had touched a lot. Not sexually, just things like holding hands, sitting super close and leaning in for a chaste but loving kiss. Like now.

He leaned in and she tipped her head up and he kissed her. Then he took hold of her hand.

At last the door opened and the doctor stepped in. He walked to his desk and sat on the leather chair with a long sigh and annoyed look at each of them.

"You two are going to have to stop dropping by unannounced. I have a practice to run."

"We wouldn't have to if we didn't keep finding out you're lying," Cal said.

"What would I have to lie about regarding Payton?"

"Why don't you just come clean, Dr. Benjamin?"

The doctor stared at him for several long seconds. "All right. Payton wasn't the one who broke things off with me. I broke them off with her."

That came as a shock. Cal kept a neutral face and hoped Jaslene was able to do the same.

"I didn't tell you because I didn't want anyone to have any reason to think I had anything to do with her disappearance."

"Why would you breaking things off instead of her make any difference? You might have been upset she broke up with you and had a reason to kidnap her, and if you broke up with her, she might have a reason to go after you."

"I can't do this anymore."

"Thanks for telling us, Doctor. Now maybe you could let us know why Payton bought a disposable phone and called the West Virginia Fraud Unit."

"She called what?" He appeared to feign ignorance,

but he blinked a few times and his tone sounded a little higher, tenser.

Cal didn't respond. The doctor had already proved himself an expert liar.

"I didn't know she bought a disposable phone."

"Oh, I think you did. Her house was searched before any police were notified of her disappearance. I bet you weren't very happy when you couldn't find the phone."

The doctor's eyes hardened. "I didn't know about any phone and this is the first I've heard about a fraud unit call."

"Now, see? That's why I think you really lied about you being the one to break up with her. You didn't want anyone to grow suspicious that she was onto you, lest they discover you had everything to do with her disappearance."

Dr. Benjamin's anger visibly increased. "This is ridiculous."

"We found her body. You may have heard about that in the news."

With that announcement, the doctor's ire faded. "Oh, that's terrible. I didn't know." Again he blinked and his tone sounded strained.

"Convenient." Until now Jaslene had been silent, letting him do all the talking.

"She was murdered," Cal said.

After a lengthy pause, Dr. Benjamin said, "And because you think I supposedly knew Payton bought a cheap phone to call a fraud unit that I must have also killed her. What good would that do me?"

"It would keep anyone from being tipped off to look into your illegal activities."

"She already called the fraud unit, based on what you just said."

"She didn't report you. I checked." Cal saw Jaslene's sharp glance his way. He'd forgotten to tell her with all the pregnancy drama going on.

"Look all you want. You won't find anything. I'm clean and I didn't kill Payton. I didn't want anything more to do with her. I decided to work on my marriage and keep my family together."

"He's lying." Jaslene stood. "Let's go."

"I'm not lying. How much do you know about her ex-boyfriend, Riley Sawyer?"

She stopped and turned to look at the doctor.

That got Cal's attention, too. "We know he's a stalker."

"I convinced her not to see him anymore." Jaslene walked back to the chair she'd vacated.

"Then it will come as no surprise to you that he stalked me, too. He threatened me not to see her anymore. One night as I was leaving the office, he appeared next to my car with a gun."

Cal believed Riley was unstable, but was the doctor using this as a tool to remove some suspicion?

"I noticed him watching us one day. We went to lunch like we frequently did and he was outside the restaurant, just standing there. That's when Payton told me about him. She was afraid because he kept spying on her." He leaned back against the chair, becoming more confident. "I asked if she'd told the police and she said Jaslene did."

"She placed a restraining order on him," Jaslene said.

Dr. Benjamin nodded. "We didn't call the police because we were afraid news of our affair would leak. A few days later, Riley met me in the parking lot and threatened me. He told me not to see Payton anymore, or else he'd tell my wife. I had to think of my family."

"That's why you broke up with her?" Jaslene asked.

The doctor nodded. "I didn't want to."

Cal didn't bother asking again why he hadn't told them this before, why he had lied. A man desperate to keep a secret would say anything to protect himself. Maybe he'd thought the lie was better than the truth, even though in this case it wasn't.

"It doesn't matter." Jaslene turned again and walked to the door.

"Riley is the one you should be looking for," Dr. Benjamin said. "I lied to keep my family together. Riley is crazy and he blames you for Payton's disappearance."

She stopped at the door.

"I'm right, aren't I?"

Cal joined Jaslene at the door.

"It's not much of a stretch to suggest Riley kidnapped Payton."

"He blames Jaslene for her death," Cal said.

"Maybe he has her all to himself now that she's dead."

"Said the man who'd say anything to throw off

suspicion." Cal put his hand on Jaslene's back and prompted her to leave.

With eyebrows low, Dr. Benjamin watched them go. He caught Cal's glance and turned away, facing his computer. But Cal knew he had only done that in an attempt to appear unaffected.

Too late.

Outside the front doors, Jaslene turned abruptly to face him. He had to take care of this now.

She put her hands on her hips. "Why didn't you tell me you called the fraud unit?"

"I'm sorry. I didn't mean not to. I've just had a lot on my mind."

After searching his face and eyes, her hands lowered to her sides. "Payton didn't report him? Why?"

"She just called to ask questions. She told them she had no proof but she heard a rumor that at least one doctor participated in a bonus program when he was employed by Dr. Benjamin. Doctors can't take kickbacks for referrals. Dr. Benjamin runs multiple practices and home health care companies. We have no way of knowing which ones participated."

Her eyes roved all over his face, full of disbelief; he could feel her injury as she absorbed what he said. "I can't believe you didn't tell me."

"I asked if they'd look into him and they said they'd sent someone to question him and the doctors at his other clinics. Nothing significant came up."

"Of course nobody's going to admit guilt on that level. Can't doctors go to jail for that?"

"And lose their medical license. I'm no expert on

that kind of law, but Dr. Benjamin could lose everything, depending on how much he swindled from the bonus program, in which he would receive money from his referrals. That chiropractor must have paid for referrals because Benjamin required that and that's why he left."

"And didn't tell anyone the truth because he paid for referrals. Benjamin had serious motive, Cal, even if the fraud unit didn't find anything. What you learned from the fraud unit, Payton's call, is huge."

Scratching his head, seeing where this was headed, he nodded. "Yeah. I thought so, too."

"And yet you didn't think to tell me."

"Jaslene." How could he explain? "The baby."

She stomped her foot. "The baby? You leave out an important detail like this and your only excuse is the *baby*?"

For a moment he could only take in the slight jiggle of her breasts and her beautiful fiery blue eyes and blond hair. "It's distracting. And I would have told you. I only just found out early this morning, when you were still sleeping. And let's not forget last night, shall we? I did have a lot on my mind, Jaslene."

All of her anger drained from her face. She contemplated him affectionately and then looped an arm around his neck, rising up to kiss him once.

Then with a twinkle in her eyes, she said, "You're forgiven," and started walking toward the SUV, heading at an angle across the parking lot lane.

"I will never understand women," he muttered low

enough for her not to hear, admiring her rear as the distance increased between them.

As he started after her, he saw a minivan approach. He paused to let the vehicle pass.

As the minivan approached Jaslene, it slowed, and before Cal could react, the side door opened and someone grabbed her, drawing her into the back seat.

"No!" he yelled, all the blood leaving his head. Not Jaslene.

He ran toward the vehicle, drawing his gun. The minivan sped away. Another car approached from the other direction, cutting him off and preventing him from firing at the tires of the minivan. Running to his SUV, he feared by the time he gave chase, it would be too late: for Jaslene, for himself and for their baby.

Jaslene screamed and kicked and tried to wrench free of her captor, who easily overpowered her. She found herself lying in the back seat of the minivan facedown, the big man cuffing her wrists behind her. Next he lifted her cell phone from her back pocket, slid down the window and threw it outside. She managed to get her knees underneath her while he was busy doing that and lifted her torso, shoving him back. She scurried to the side of the minivan, seeing part of the driver's face in the rearview mirror. It was Riley.

The big man jammed a gun against her ribs. "Don't move again."

Jaslene studied his face. He had blocky features, a big nose and square jaw and thick brow. His dark hair was shaved millimeter short. He had a winged tattoo on his left forearm, the hand that held the gun. He was left-handed.

She glanced around. The minivan windows were darkly tinted in the back. She recognized the road and realized they were heading for Webster Springs. She looked behind them and saw no sign of Cal's SUV. She was in trouble.

Okay. She had to stay calm. Her racing heart and imaginings of what harm might come to her made it difficult to keep the fear at bay. *Think.*

As they reached the outskirts of Webster Springs, Riley turned on a side street. They passed a few houses and came to a trailer park, where they turned in.

She was running out of time. If Riley got her wherever he intended to take her, she was finished.

Riley stopped next to a trailer at the end of a row of them.

"Make a sound when we get out and I'll shoot you," Riley said as he climbed out of the driver's seat and slammed the door shut.

He opened the back door and showed her the gun he also held. The big man got out, closed the door and went to the other side, standing next to Riley. Keeping his gun on Jaslene, Riley pulled out an envelope from inside his black leather jacket and handed it to the big man, who took it and walked toward another car parked on the street in front of the trailer.

"If you try anything, I'll kill you now. I don't care if I get caught. You either die now or you buy yourself some time by not fighting me."

That was terrifying. She believed him. He obviously didn't care if he was caught.

Jaslene looked around. No one was outside and no cars passed on the street.

"Get out. I won't tell you again."

Jaslene did as he said. He pressed the gun to her side as his hired thug drove off without a single look her way.

She faced the trailer, each step toward the door feeling like another one closer to her death. Would he shoot her as soon as he had her inside? He must care whether he'd be caught or he'd have already tried to kill her. He also wouldn't have hired anyone to help him snatch her and bring her here.

She wanted to fight and try to escape, but with her hands cuffed like this her chances were slim. And the baby. If she was hurt, the baby might be hurt as well.

Scared and fighting to stay focused, she climbed the steps.

"Open the door."

She opened the door, which he had left unlocked. Then he pushed her inside. It was dim, with two windows providing meager light in the small space.

"Down the hall."

"Why are you doing this?" She walked slowly.

He shoved her into a faster gait. "You know why."

"I didn't cause Payton's murder."

"You caused us to split up." He grabbed her arm and steered her into the second doorway. She saw two locks in a heavy door. This room had a twin bed and a single window with bars.

He pushed her and she fell to her knees.

"I didn't cause your split. Payton would have broken up with you anyway. You have to see that."

"She would be safe with me right now if it hadn't been for your meddling. You talked her into ending it with me. Now you're going to pay." He removed the handcuffs.

Jaslene stood and faced him, rubbing her wrists.

"What did you do with Payton?" she asked.

"I loved her." He moved to the bed, making Jaslene cringe. But he only picked up some rope.

"Enough to kill her?" She eyed the rope, wondering if it was the same that had been used to tie a cement block to Payton's ankles.

"I didn't kill her. That doctor did."

Jaslene perked up at that. "How do you know?"

He paused in unwinding the rope, which had gotten tangled. "I saw him park his car at the park around the corner from her house. I didn't recognize him. I didn't know she was seeing him until I saw you and that detective at his clinic. It dawned on me that he must have gone to her house that night I saw him."

So, Dr. Benjamin lied about Riley threatening him. "Why not go to the police? You could identify her killer." She moved back as far as she could. He must intend to tie her up in this room.

"Oh, I'll make sure he pays, too. But first you."

What did he plan to do? "Why were you at the park that night?" He could be lying the same way Dr. Benjamin had. He could be Payton's killer.

"I wasn't at the park. I had just left Payton's. She

wasn't home yet, so I left and as I drove past the park, I saw a man get out of a Mercedes and start walking in the direction of Payton's house. I got a good look at his face. I'm really good with that, remembering faces. I figured out who he was later." He untangled one four-foot length of rope and started to untangle the other.

Jaslene eyed his gun, which he still aimed at her as he worked. Should she kick his hand? "You didn't come back?"

"I did, the next morning. When she didn't leave for work, I drove to her work and she wasn't there, either. I knew something was wrong then, and the next day I found out she had been reported missing." He stopped what he was doing to look at her. "I looked everywhere for her. Everywhere. I broke into her house to see if I could find any clues, too."

"Did you leave her house a mess?"

"No. There were subtle signs that someone had been through it, though. I thought the police must have already been there."

So he hadn't been the one to search her house. That had to have been Dr. Benjamin.

He lowered his head. "I knew something bad must have happened to her. I knew she must have been killed." He looked at her again. "I mourned for weeks and weeks. And then I realized if it hadn't been for you, she'd still be here. She'd be in my arms, safe."

"Riley, that is ridiculous. We found out Dr. Benjamin is involved in some type of insurance fraud and Payton knew about it. He is the one who killed her. Cal and I are going to prove it."

Riley stared at her for long seconds. "I know that. Didn't you hear me?"

She hoped to make him somehow see reason. "He's the one who should be punished."

He resumed untangling the rope, mostly one-handed. "Payton should have never been with him."

Did he think Payton had made the mistake of being unfaithful to him? That if she had never left Riley, she'd have never had the affair with the doctor? Since he blamed Jaslene for their breakup, he'd assigned all the guilt for Payton's death to her in his twisted mind.

"Why not just kill me now if you're so convinced I'm at fault?" she asked, hoping the tactic wouldn't backfire.

"That's not enough punishment for you. I want you to suffer the way Payton must have suffered because of you, the way you've made me suffer." He gestured toward the head of the twin bed. "Get on the bed."

Her heart lurched in fear. She had to do something now or she'd never get another chance. If he tied her to that headboard, she'd endure unimaginable horrors.

Beside himself with fear for Jaslene, Cal had to force himself to stay focused. He'd contacted experts at DAI, who had tracked Jaslene's cell phone to a location outside of town, in the direction of Webster Springs. Riley had used his own name to rent a trailer.

Cal refused to wait for police and raced there now. All Cal cared about was saving Jaslene and their baby. If anything happened to either one of them, he'd be more devastated than he'd been when he'd discovered his ex-wife's treachery. He'd ponder that once he had Jaslene safe and in his arms.

He came to the turn to the trailer park and switched off his headlights, taking the long way around in case anyone was keeping watch. Riley had found someone to help him kidnap Jaslene. While Cal doubted he'd pay the thug to stick around to hurt her, he wouldn't take any chances.

It was getting late in the day and the sun had begun to set. Today had been a clear day, with no more snow in the forecast for at least a few more days.

Cal parked a few trailers down from Riley's address, readied his guns—he'd brought three—and alighted from the SUV. He'd changed into more tactical clothes, all black, so he couldn't be seen approaching.

Checking his surroundings, making sure he wouldn't be caught, he made it to the side of the trailer, opposite the front door. He moved quietly along. Light illuminated windows. The first had bars on it. He could see Riley's and Jaslene's shadows on a cheap shade. The second didn't have bars, just a closed shade. Rising up, he peered through a crack in the blind. He saw nothing at first, then the curve of a hip and a glimpse of blond hair.

"No," he heard her say.

She was alive.

Lowering his head, he breathed in profound relief.

Then he thought of the best way to go in and get her. Riley was in the room with her.

He hurried to the back of the trailer and found a

back door. He made quick work of picking the old lock and was in.

His gun ready, he moved stealthily down the hall to the room with the barred window. The door was ajar. He kicked it open and shouted, "Drop your gun now!"

Riley held a rope and a pistol and jumped, startled by the interruption. At the same time, Jaslene ducked and dived toward the side of the room, away from Riley's gun.

Riley started to turn the gun on Cal, who shot him in his shoulder. As Riley dropped his weapon, Cal rushed to him, putting a knee in the small of his back. Kicking Riley's gun away, Cal aimed his pistol at his forehead.

"I should kill you right now."

"Cal, no. Let the police arrest him. He knows Dr. Benjamin was at the park. Riley saw him."

That hit Cal like a bull's-eye.

She handed him handcuffs. "He had these on me."

Cal took them and yanked Riley so he was face-down and then bent his arms behind his back. Riley cried out in pain, his shoulder bloody. Cal cuffed him. Then he used the rope he would have used on Jaslene to tie his feet.

Riley moaned on the floor.

Cal stood and turned to Jaslene. He went to her and took her into his arms.

"I just have to hold you." He embraced her firmly, smelling her hair, kissing her ear, her forehead. "You have no idea."

"You have no idea how glad I am you got here when you did."

"I do. I do." He leaned back and kissed her mouth, then held her face between his hands and looked at her.

She smiled shakily. "Get me out of here."

"With pleasure."

Chapter 16

With Riley now under arrest and the police hot on his accomplice's tail, Jaslene and Cal were able to zero in on Dr. Benjamin. She sat with him at the table after sharing a light breakfast, finishing her second cup of decaffeinated coffee, the next morning. She still felt tired after everything she had been through. She just wanted all of this to be over so she could turn all her attention to Cal and the baby.

"That masked hit man needs to be found. He isn't Riley's accomplice," he said.

That could go without mention. "Benjamin isn't going to tell us anything."

"We still have no proof, but if the warrant is approved, Forensics can search his Mercedes."

It didn't seem like they had enough evidence for

a judge to grant a search warrant. "Maybe we should talk to that other doctor again, the one that left Benjamin's organization."

He looked up from his laptop, a steaming cup of coffee nearby and his light blue eyes zinging her with their attractiveness and the affection that was always there. She also noticed that his tight black, long-sleeved undershirt accentuated his muscular arms and chest.

"It's worth a try." He reached over and put his hand on hers, the feelings between them warming.

A flutter of wariness flashed as worry over whether this emotion would last came over her. She loved these sweet, innocent moments with him but they drew her to him inexorably. How nice it would be to completely let go and fall completely.

How close he'd come, or how close he *perceived* he'd come, to losing her made him this attentive. Or was it because he truly cared for her?

"Shall we go?" She slid her hand away and stood.

His warmth turned to concern. He stood and came to her.

"You've been a little skittish with me today. Why?"

He had to ask? "I'm just…still out of sorts with us."

"Don't you trust me?"

How could she answer that and be completely honest? "I don't know."

His gaze grew more intense and he put his hands on her upper arms. "Let's not look ahead anymore, Jaslene. Let's take one day at a time."

She supposed she could do that, but what if one day she let her guard down and really fell for him, only to discover on said day that he couldn't be with her long-term? She'd already had her heart broken with Ryan. She had to at least try to protect herself from another.

"One day at a time," he said again.

She nodded a few times, unable to meet his eyes again.

Cal waited with Jaslene at Dr. Faulkner's office. All he had to do was concentrate on today, and today they would talk to the chiropractor. Unfortunately, he also couldn't stop concentrating on Jaslene. In a warm, soft black sweater dress, tights and boots, she looked so feminine and sexy.

The doctor finally entered the office. "I'm so sorry to keep you waiting." He strode to his desk and sat, running his fingers through his salt-and-pepper hair. "It's been a busy day."

"Thank you for seeing us," Cal said, not missing how much more genuine his tone was than Benjamin's.

The doctor adjusted his glasses. "I'm not sure I can help you."

The last time they talked, Dr. Faulkner had said Dr. Benjamin would have liked to have his referrals. "We discovered something new about Dr. Benjamin. You had mentioned not approving of his ethics. We have good reason to believe he was involved in a fraudulent referral program. Did you ever refer any patients to Dr. Benjamin's clinics?" Cal asked.

Dr. Faulkner met Cal's eyes for several long seconds. "Once."

"Is that why you left?"

He nodded. "Yes. I didn't know at the time that Dr. Benjamin would be paid for my referrals. There was nothing about them in my contract. I resigned from Dr. Benjamin's organization immediately. I already had a decent following of patients. Dr. Benjamin wasn't very happy about that. He lost revenue. After a few months, though, I gained revenue."

Dr. Benjamin wanted his referrals. It occurred to Cal that Dr. Faulkner had never told them how he'd explained his resignation to Dr. Benjamin. "What reason did you give him?"

"I only told him I'd decided to go out on my own. I felt bringing up the referrals or his unethical relations with patients would only stir up trouble for me. I figured if he took risks like that, he'd pay for them on his own. I didn't want to be part of his operation anymore."

Benjamin hadn't been clued in to the real reason why Faulkner left. Otherwise, surely he'd have gone after Faulkner, too.

"At the time I didn't know about Payton," the doctor continued. "It never dawned on me that Dr. Benjamin would be involved. How did you make the connection?"

"Payton called the fraud unit prior to her murder."

"Murder?"

"Yes. Her body was recently found."

The doctor's head lowered and a remorseful sigh blew from slightly parted lips. "That's terrible."

Cal gave him a moment. "Dr. Faulkner, we can't solve her murder without evidence. You have information that can lead us to that evidence. Are you willing to provide that and possibly testify in court?"

The doctor lifted his head. "I'll do whatever you need me to do."

"Then let's start with you telling us everything you know about his business practices."

Dr. Faulkner nodded. "He does more than promote an internal referral program. He routinely does tests and orders procedures that aren't necessary on his patients. Not invasive surgeries, but things like EKGs, X-rays and blood tests to get more money from insurance."

"How can we prove that?" Jaslene asked, looking at Cal.

"You would need to get copies of his files," Dr. Faulkner said. "I think your best bet would be to get records from one of his home health care facilities. He makes most of his money there, ordering home care for patients that don't really need it. I never referred patients there, but I do have a lot that I could. Dr. Benjamin liked my older patients. Thank goodness I left before he could get to them."

Payton had died before she could find concrete evidence of fraud. She never got the chance.

Cal looked over at Jaslene, who seemed to study the chiropractor in somber thought. She'd likely drawn the same conclusions.

"What are you going to do?" the doctor asked. "Will you report me?"

He feared his mistake in referring one patient to Dr. Benjamin's empire. Cal would set his mind at ease.

"No. We want Benjamin, not you. Besides that, I'm

not a cop." Cal stood and extended his hand. "Thank you very much, Doctor."

Dr. Faulkner shook his hand. "Thank you."

Jaslene stood, a smooth, graceful move, and said, "Payton was a good friend of mine. I've been waiting a long time for a break in this case. You just might have given us the one we need. Now we have a clear motive."

"Well, if so, be careful. Dr. Benjamin would go far to protect his criminal activities, since your friend is dead. You could be in danger."

Faulkner must have feared the same when he'd left Benjamin's organization. "He's already come after us, through a hired gunman," Cal said. "If I was him, I'd be on the run right now. His secret is out."

What would a desperate man do once he realized police not only had a body, but motive as well?

"You know if you report him you get a percentage of whatever the government recovers from their investigation?" Cal asked.

"No. Really?"

"File a whistle-blower lawsuit with the fraud unit," Jaslene said.

She clearly wanted Benjamin to pay.

"I'll think about it. But I must say, I care more about my patients and my peaceful life than I do about my relations with Dr. Benjamin. Frankly, I wish I'd have never met him."

Cal wished Payton had never met him, too.

The next night, Jaslene listened to Cal on the phone with his police contact as they neared the building of a local home care administrative center. The evening before, they'd scoped out the center and saw the last janitor leave around 10:00 p.m. Fifteen minutes from now.

She wore black leggings with a short black cotton shirt and a black leather jacket. Cal also wore dark jeans, boots, Henley and his own bulkier leather jacket.

Cal disconnected his call. "They finally got his wife to talk. Dr. Benjamin took his wife to dinner the night Payton went missing. Police detectives confirmed they arrived at eight forty-five."

"That's a late dinner."

"He left work at six. That gives him two hours and forty-five minutes before dinner. Plenty of time to drive to the park, walk to Payton's and carry out his crime."

"And then have a nice dinner with his wife." Jaslene scoffed. "Who could do that?"

"Someone without a conscience. A narcissist."

Good people could never relate to that way of thinking or physical violence. She imagined him moving Payton's body. "I can't believe no one saw him transfer her body from her car to his at the park."

"It gets pretty dark." Plus there were a lot of trees. "Parks are a popular place for killers and rapists," Cal said.

"Where is Dr. Benjamin?"

"They were on their way to pick him up for questioning."

At last. Payton's death would be avenged. By the time they got out of this building with evidence, the police could arrest Dr. Benjamin. Of course, they weren't really going to break in. The janitor had agreed to allow them access. Earlier today, Cal had discovered the janitor's sister worked for Dr. Benjamin, who had made inappropriate advances on her, and he wanted justice.

The janitor appeared, looking toward them and waving them in.

She walked with Cal to the short, skinny man with a sandy-blond ponytail who held the door for them.

"All you have to do is leave through this door. It will lock automatically," the janitor said.

"Thanks."

The janitor looked left to right as he walked toward his vehicle as Cal held the door for Jaslene. He then led the way through the building, locating the area where the janitor had said insurance claims and patient files were kept. Jaslene went to a computer that hadn't yet gone into sleep mode where she could access the patient files and sat down for a long study. Cal found a laptop and came back to sit next to her, starting to search insurance claims.

"Look up Andrew Simpson," he said after almost an hour. She did.

"Office visit for a cold."

"Billed as an extensive visit with pneumonia." He gave her another name.

"Emergency for a head wound. Stitches were put in."

"Billed as emergency life support transportation. The stitching was billed with three different codes. Unbundling is illegal. There's another one in here where the same procedure was billed more than once."

"We've got him."

Jaslene looked at his smiling face and beamed one back at him.

Cal started saving files and taking pictures. "The police will get a search warrant but let's copy a few examples just in case."

She saved a few files and he came over to the computer she'd borrowed to look them up and took pictures.

"Let's get out of here." They'd started to leave when a sudden sound alerted Jaslene they weren't alone.

Cal looked over the top of cubicle walls. Jaslene wasn't tall enough to see, but she knew he'd spotted someone.

He took her hand and pulled out his gun at the same time. "This way." He led her, crouched below the level of the walls, the opposite direction. The problem was, the door they needed was in the same direction as the intruder. Had Dr. Benjamin caught them somehow?

Cal turned down another cubicle hallway and stopped, positioning himself at the corner and her next to him. Slowly, he peered first into the hallway and then raised his head over the wall. He looked in a full circle and must not have spotted anyone, since he led her on.

Jaslene checked behind them and saw nothing. But then a man appeared at the other end of the hallway.

"Cal!" She pushed him and he turned, hauling her in front of him and then ducking around another corner.

"He's not there anymore."

He wasn't firing any gunshots. "Is it Dr. Benjamin?"

"Yes." He took her hand again. "Come on."

He ran down another hall. This one would lead them to the door heading outside—if they could make it.

Reaching the end of the cubicle area, Cal pulled her down an office-lined hall and eventually to the warehouse area where they'd entered.

The intruder didn't chase them.

Once outside, Cal kept checking behind them as they sprinted to his SUV. There, he stopped her, quickly checking the car's undercarriage for any signs of tampering.

She alighted into the now unlocked vehicle, staring at the building, searching for their pursuer, who must be Dr. Benjamin. He never appeared.

"Why didn't he shoot at us?" she asked.

"Evidence. He didn't want bullets or holes."

"Why did he chase us?"

"I don't think he did. He must have just wanted to see who was there."

"Well, surely he must know it would be us."

"Or someone working late."

Which he certainly must have hoped. Now he knew it was them, that they'd likely found what he'd tried so hard to hide.

Back at home, Jaslene relaxed with Rapunzel. Cal's police friend had come to take what they'd found at the office, but recorded a legitimate version of how they'd obtained it. His story left a few things out—namely, Dr. Benjamin chasing them—or not chasing them.

There would be a search warrant ordered for Dr. Benjamin's offices and also his house and Mercedes. Jaslene was most interested in what Forensics would find in the car, since Payton's body had been moved. Maybe there would be trace evidence in there.

Sitting on the sofa next to Cal, a documentary playing on the television that she wasn't really paying attention to, she pet Rapunzel's head.

The puppy's eyes rolled over to Cal, her head tipping back and to the side, the picture of spoiled rotten.

Cal chuckled at the sight. "Is that what you're going to do with our baby?"

She loved how his voice sounded, especially when he said "our."

"And then some."

Chapter 17

Cal woke in the morning to his mobile phone ringing. A split second later he felt Jaslene's body pressed along his side and Rapunzel had her chin on his shoulder. The dog had curled up on the pillow beside him sometime during the night.

He sat up, disturbing Rapunzel enough to make her move closer to Jaslene, who had also begun to stir.

"Chelsey."

"Hey." It was a Chesterville Police Department detective. "We got Benjamin's hit man. Chaz Mendel. He has a rap sheet two miles long. Full of robberies, restraining orders, a couple of assaults. Did five in prison a few years back."

Cal put the phone on speaker as Jaslene blinked sleep out of her eyes and scooted back against the headboard to sit up. Rapunzel decided to vacate the active bed and jumped down for the quieter comfort of her dog bed.

"That's excellent news," Cal said, then to Jaslene, he murmured, "They got Benjamin's hired hit man to talk."

"He talked when we offered a lighter sentence. He must know how it works, which is why he's spent so much time free," the detective said.

"What about the search warrants?"

"We're picking up the Mercedes as we speak. Teams are going through all of Dr. Benjamin's records at his company—all locations, and the search of his house has commenced. Mendel said he paid him ten grand to help him kidnap Jaslene. Doc didn't tell him why and he didn't ask. He wasn't much help beyond that and agreeing to testify."

When he had first knocked Jaslene out and started the fire, he must have intended to take care of Cal so he wouldn't go after him after he kidnapped Jaslene. When that didn't work he decided to just kidnap her and lure Cal so he could take care of him later. Maybe he thought the fire would cover his tracks, get rid of Cal's body.

"Okay. What about the missus?" Cal asked.

"I'm here at the house now and was one of the first to go in. She's pretty rattled. She had no idea what her husband was doing."

"Where's Benjamin?"

"Not home and not at the office."

"He ran."

"That would be my assumption as well." The detective sounded disappointed, but not nearly as much as Jaslene looked.

Dr. Benjamin was on the run, which meant this was not over yet.

The doorbell rang. Cal checked his phone. They'd slept late.

"Who would be here at this hour?" Jaslene asked, starting to get out of bed.

"You go ahead and shower. I'll get the door." He pulled on the jeans he'd had on last night and headed downstairs.

Before opening the door, he peered out the side window and experienced a shock. His parents were out there.

Opening the door, he couldn't form any words.

His mother smiled huge and his father grinned.

"Good morning, son." His mother leaned in for a kiss to his cheek and a hug. She seemed full of energy, back to herself, which was nice to see.

"What are you doing here?" he finally found his thoughts to ask.

"We wanted to surprise you. We've never been here and you weren't answering your phone at your house."

"How did you find me?"

"Your boss told me where you were staying," his dad said.

They entered the house, his mother taking in the interior and his father carrying a small luggage. They didn't appear to plan to stay long.

"You could have told us your house burned down."

His mother faced him and his father put down the luggage and did the same.

"It has some damage. I'm repairing it." He followed them into the living room. "We were unharmed."

"Still. You could have called."

"You're right. I'm sorry. I'm in the middle of a case."

"If we're going to change the way things have gone in the past, the communication needs to stay open," his mother went on.

Normally it would have been his dad laying into him. But he now realized he'd hurt his mother by not calling since his visit. He might have seen it as unimportant since no one was hurt in the fire, but she saw it as a slight.

"I'll have to get used to that. I will." He went to her and put his hands on her arms. "I promise."

Her eyes went soft and she kissed his cheek again. "Okay, good. Now, where is that girl of yours? I didn't get a chance to really talk to her when you came to Texas."

"She's getting ready."

Cal's parents left yesterday, after staying for two days. The detective Cal had been working with called. Jaslene listened in. Although official results were still pending, fibers found in the Mercedes appeared to match those found embedded in what remained of Payton's clothes. Even better, the rope recovered from the crime scene matched the type Dr. Benjamin had purchased from a hardware store not long before Payton's disappearance. And on the more mysterious side, the doctor's wife, Sarah, seemed to be withholding information on her husband's whereabouts.

Detectives asked her again about the last time she'd seen him and she had changed her story. First she'd said she'd last seen him the morning Cal and Jaslene had gone searching for fraud evidence at his office. Then just today she'd claimed she'd last seen him at home the night Cal and Jaslene ran from him at the health care administrative office building. So, clearly she was lying.

Cal told the detective they'd give her a try next. Maybe if she wasn't talking to cops she'd open up a little more. Maybe she was just afraid. Sarah had remained locked up in her house and had changed all the locks, a pretty good indication she was afraid.

By that afternoon, Jaslene stood with Cal before a grand double entry with side windows and another above the doors. Dr. Benjamin's house was nothing short of spectacular, a small-scale but beautiful mansion located in the most prestigious neighborhood in Chesterville.

A maid answered.

"Hello. We're here to see Mrs. Benjamin," Jaslene said.

"She isn't taking any visitors."

"Please, would you tell her a friend of Payton Everett is here?"

The maid opened the door and let them into a giant entry with towering ceiling and elaborate chandelier. "Wait here."

About five minutes passed before Mrs. Benjamin

appeared through the double doors. She stopped when she saw Cal.

"I'm a private detective Jaslene hired to help find her friend, Payton," Cal said.

The woman, who looked as impeccably groomed as her husband, if not more so, extended her arm to the gaudy but surely authentic parlor. "Why don't we go in there."

Jaslene sat next to Cal on a handcrafted Victorian settee. Mrs. Benjamin sat across from them in one of two green, wood-trimmed wingback chairs.

"I heard about that girl and that my husband might be responsible for her disappearance and her…" She put her hand to her mouth as though to stave off a rush of tears. When she regained composure, she said, "I can't believe he'd do such a thing."

"Who told you he might be responsible?" Cal asked.

Jaslene recalled police weren't revealing much about the body found, but the news had since released her name once Payton's family had been notified.

"The police have been questioning me."

Jaslene leaned forward with her forearms on her knees. "Mrs. Benjamin, we know this is very difficult for you, but we now know your husband was involved with Payton's disappearance and most likely her murder. If there's anything you can tell us about where we can find him, we can all put this behind us."

"My kids…"

"They're going to find out eventually anyway. You can't protect them from what will happen with or without your help. Your husband will be arrested and most likely charged with kidnapping and murder. Your kids aren't going to see him outside of prison."

"You can't say that for certain."

"We have evidence, Mrs. Benjamin," Cal said. "Fiber evidence that links your husband to the crime scene. He'll be arrested and charged. His trial will determine his sentence."

"Oh." Mrs. Benjamin stood and walked to the front window with one hand on her hip. She wiped her cheek with her other hand, an indication she shed a few quiet tears.

She was another victim of Dr. John Benjamin's wrongdoings.

"The last time I saw him was late at night four days ago. He packed a small bag. He took a passport out of his office safe and told me he had arranged for us to live in another city under different names. He denied having anything to do with that woman and assured me he'd be back for me." She wiped her cheek again. "I believed him, but, truthfully, I've been so confused these last few days. I truly don't know my own husband. The man I married isn't who I thought he was."

She turned to face them, lowering her arms to her sides. "Just this morning I went to the hotel in Charleston to meet him. When I arrived there, I discovered he'd never checked in, but I showed the clerk a picture and she said he did check in but under another name. He has been running a practice under a different name. I called in a favor from a friend, who located his house. I went there and saw him with another woman. It explained so much. All the time he was gone from home, he wasn't working at his other clinics. He was living another life in another city with another woman."

And with another practice. Jaslene turned to Cal in utter amazement. Had that been his escape plan? He must have spent a lot of time and painstaking calculation in setting up such a wild scheme.

"From the looks of them, they'd been together for at least several years. They had a young boy with them, presumably their son, maybe about five. He was there with them."

Jaslene stood and went to the poor woman. She gave her a brief, comforting hug. "I'm so sorry."

"Family was so important to him." She no longer tried to curb her tears. She sobbed a few times.

"I believe family was important to him. When we spoke to him he told us how important you were. You and his kids, his family."

Her crying eased and she searched Jaslene's eyes for truth.

"My impression of him was he'd go to any length to protect that, to make sure he could still have that with you, be it here or in another city. I think you can believe he's working right now to find you a new house where you can all live under his new name."

Mrs. Benjamin seemed to undergo a moment of clarity. Her eyes cleared of hurt and she took a step away from Jaslene.

"I can't do that," she said, incredulous.

And that's when Jaslene knew she'd cooperate with the police.

Chapter 18

After leaving Mrs. Benjamin, Cal walked with Jaslene up to Claypoole Medical Center. It was a narrow red-brick building with big white pillars marking the front entrance. Off Virginia Street East, it was a short walk to the Kanawha River. Under a pretty blue sky, the Charleston street oozed small-town charm, everything Cal loved about a place.

"If things go south in there, I want you to wait in the SUV," Cal said, his long strides gobbling up Jaslene's.

"I won't run after him, if that's what you mean."

"I need you to be safe. There's more than you we have to worry about." He'd die if anything happened to her or the baby.

"You're the one with the gun," she said as he reached the door. "What about the police?"

"I will call them after we have Benjamin. I want this wrapped up."

She went in first. The reception area wasn't large but had new dark mosaic carpeting and wood-framed antique waiting room chairs. Very nice. Everything he'd expect from a man like Benjamin. Stiff and staged.

Cal waited for the receptionist to finish with a patient and then asked to see the doctor.

"Do you have an appointment?"

"No."

"I'm sorry, he's seeing patients right now."

Cal turned to Jaslene. "Call 911 and wait here."

She nodded and then he pushed through the door to the back of the office and walked down a hallway.

"Sir?" The receptionist chased after him. "You can't go back there."

He shrugged off her hand when she put it on his biceps. Rather than intrude on innocent people behind closed doors, he stopped at each closed door to listen.

"Sir!"

He turned a corner and spotted Dr. Benjamin coming out of a room.

Benjamin saw him and stopped short, his eyes widening. Then he dropped the chart he held and ran the other way.

"Stop!" Cal ran after him.

The doctor slammed through double swinging doors. Cal banged into the break room after him, a nurse shrieking and jumping out of the way. Dr. Benjamin dashed through a back door, Cal just behind him.

The doctor was in really good shape. He sprinted

through a parking lot behind the office building. Removing the white lab coat that flapped with his movements, he tossed it aside. Seeing he packed a gun in a holster, which had been hidden by the long medical jacket, Cal drew his own weapon.

The doctor twisted his body as he ran. Cal ducked behind a parked car as Benjamin fired. Then he resumed his chase. The doctor left the parking lot for an alley running between a row of old houses. Cal sprinted past narrow backyards. Some had detached one-car garages and others had attached garages. A dog barked and charged one fence.

Benjamin hopped the fence of a yard two houses down. Cal leaped it after him and gained a little ground until the doctor tipped over a grill to block his path.

Cal nearly tripped over the grill and managed to crouch before Benjamin fired his gun again. He disappeared through the back door of the house. His motion smooth, as though he'd planned this in case he needed to escape.

Cautiously, Cal entered the house. He heard Benjamin knocking something over in the kitchen. Aiming his pistol, Cal cleared the wall and spotted the doctor going into the garage. He rushed to the garage door as Benjamin slammed it shut.

Cal opened the door.

Dr. Benjamin got into a BMW.

Cal shot the front and rear tires out and then aimed at Benjamin's head. "It's over. Get your hands up."

Raising his gun, Dr. Benjamin fired back as Cal

went low. The garage door began to open. He was not making this easy on Cal.

"You aren't going anywhere, Dr. Benjamin. We know all about you."

"I'll kill you!"

The doctor was determined to get away. He refused to acknowledge that he'd lost, that his crime had been exposed along with his fake identity.

Cal would have to act. He rose quickly, seeing the doctor still had his weapon aimed. He fired, true and fast, hitting the doctor's hand.

Benjamin yelped and dropped the gun, giving Cal a chance to get to the door, which was still open, and haul the man out and drag Dr. Benjamin onto the concrete floor of the garage. He stumbled to his feet, holding his bleeding hand. Still slightly bent over, the doctor spat, "You son of a bitch!" as he rammed into Cal. Cal stepped back as the doctor straightened and took a swing with his good hand.

Cal easily blocked his arm and ended the attempted punch, then brought his gun-free fist up into his sternum. Benjamin grunted and struggled for breath, but still had some fight in him. He grabbed Cal's legs and plowed forward. Cal went down but not for long. He used his legs to maneuver free of Benjamin's hold, ending up on his knees, straddling the man. He hit his pistol against Benjamin's head.

Dr. Benjamin collapsed back down, dazed and blinking unsteadily.

Rising to his feet, Cal kept his gun steady and said, "Get up."

Looking up at him and the gun aimed between his eyes, a moment later defeat settled in. He climbed to his feet, hand dripping blood.

"Was it worth it?" Cal asked.

Dr. Benjamin said nothing.

"Hands behind your back."

He did as ordered and Cal moved to cuff him. "You would have still made a decent living without the fraud. Why do it?"

"I wouldn't have made enough to expand."

"I wonder." If he'd have given it more time, certainly he would have expanded his operation. He had the drive, the means and the business acumen.

Cal moved in front of him again. "Was this your escape if you needed it or did you just get your rocks off fooling everyone?"

"You wouldn't understand."

"The mind of a madman? No." He grabbed the doctor's shoulder and propelled him into a walk. "I just wanted to know if it was all worth it."

The doctor walked without comment.

When they reached the parking lot, a flock of police cars surrounded the front entrance and blocked the street. Emergency vehicles waited farther down, at a safe distance.

"Why Payton?" Cal asked before they reached the throng. "She didn't know anything."

"What about Payton?"

"You can cut the bull now. We all know everything." He spotted Jaslene standing among the police officers.

She turned her head and saw them and her shoulders sunk in what must be relief.

Was she relieved to see him or to see that he had Dr. Benjamin?

Several policemen approached.

"We got word from the Chesterville Police Department that you were looking for their suspect," the first to stop before them said. "He'll be transported to that jurisdiction."

"Thanks."

Jaslene came to stand beside Cal, staring at Dr. Benjamin as the policeman took control of him and he faced her and Cal.

"Why?" she all but breathed.

Dr. Benjamin's face didn't change, as though he felt no remorse for all he'd done. It was clear that his only regret was getting caught.

She took a step forward, looked him straight in the eyes and then slapped him.

Dr. Benjamin's head moved left and he turned back to her without flinching.

Without another word, she walked away.

Jaslene took a day to mourn Payton. It hadn't really hit her that her friend was dead. For so long she'd hoped she wouldn't be. And she'd been so busy with the investigation. Now everything had been turned over to police and they would take it from here. She had to face the reality: Payton was gone. Dead. Murdered by a no-good, greedy and evil secret lover. Incomprehension morphed into stark emotion and that led to anger.

The urge to pound both fists on the table nearly got the better of her.

That gradually passed as Jaslene no longer denied her loss. Payton died and Jaslene could accept that now. She'd always be sad. She'd always miss her good friend. But she could hold on to the good memories.

What Dr. Benjamin had done would always anger her. She'd never understand why he had taken such a good soul. But he would never tarnish her memories.

Standing from the dining room chair, she left her steaming cup of herbal tea and walked through her kitchen, plagued by the truth gnawing at her core. *Soul mate.* She had never experienced that wonder before and didn't know what to do with it now.

Embrace it? Him? Could she trust?

It all seemed so daunting.

Would he ever trust her? She didn't want to be the one to try to *fix* him. She didn't believe men who were that broken *could* be fixed. But maybe he wasn't broken at all. Maybe he only needed to be shown the way. Maybe he'd already seen it.

Jaslene was ready to give love another try. Real love. She wouldn't throw away an opportunity because she feared…something—Cal not reciprocating, failing again at marriage—losing another person she loved.

She didn't go to college and get a difficult job because she was a quitter.

The absurd urge to be back in Cal's house struck her. She wanted it refurbished. Her house was too functional. Not enough charm. Not that Cal's had charm in

the way of decor. The things that made a family—to-
kens, sentimental pieces—were missing.

"I have something to show you."

Jaslene nearly jumped out of her skin. She turned
to see Cal in the entry of the kitchen, in his jacket and
holding keys.

"Let's go."

In black jeans and sturdy boots again, he gave her
a whole-body tingle, especially those sexy, mischie-
vous blue eyes.

Where did he plan to take her?

"Bring Rapunzel."

Cal would never forget the way Jaslene looked when
he'd come into her kitchen, ready to take her to his
home. Peace had haloed her, peace from grief that had
run its course and left bittersweet memories. And inner
strength. Loss would not bring her down. Maybe she
had just realized that. He hoped so. He also hoped she
had forgiven herself for reacting to Ansel. And him,
for doubting her.

After parking in the driveway of his house, Cal got
out before Jaslene could voice her startled and questioning look. Rapunzel helped his cause by pawing
her a couple of times.

He jogged around to her side and opened the door.
Rapunzel pawed her again, lying half on her and half
on the seat.

Cal leaned down, one hand on the top of the SUV.
"That dog is getting too big for your lap."

"No, she isn't."

"You're going to ruin a good herding animal."

Jaslene put one hand on his chest and pushed gently. He took the hint and moved back.

She stood and walked with the puppy by her side to the front door.

She reached the door and stopped, waiting for him, coy eyes and a soft smile. Rapunzel joined in with intermittent round-eyed innocence mixed with sleepy droops.

Cal opened the door, having to fight to hold on to trust.

She stepped inside, thrilled that he had made her wish come true. "You renovated quickly."

He waited for her to notice all the changes. The main living area had suffered the most damage. Instead of going back to gray and white, he'd hired an interior decorator, who'd done the living room in teal and white. Eye-catching, color coordinated paintings now hung on the walls. Other accents made the room homey. The kitchen had been redone pretty much the same as it looked before, with gray cabinetry and white-topped stools. Fresh flowers were on the dining room table.

But this wasn't what he wanted her to see.

"Nice," she said.

"Come with me." He led her up the stairs.

She followed him to one of the rooms he'd finished furnishing. Rapunzel trotted along behind them. At the room, Jaslene slowed as she entered, passing him. It contained a crib, dresser and diaper changing station.

"It needs to be painted and decorated," he said. "After we know if we're having a boy or a girl." He figured the gesture would be enough to let her know his plans. He'd wrestled with it for a few days and finally came to the conclusion he'd be a fool to drive her away. She was genuine and honest. He had to believe that this time he would get it right.

"You really want to do this?" She faced him.

He understood what she asked. She needed the unvarnished truth. "I am sure. I'm also sure that I need to learn how to trust again. I know I can trust you."

"You just need to convince your heart?"

"Yes." He grinned. "It might seem silly but…"

"No." She stepped closer and put her hands on his chest. "You were married to a woman who deceived you. You gave her your love and trust and she betrayed that. It's like me losing Ryan. It took me a long time to stop overprotecting my heart from more pain. It might seem absurd to some but when someone close dies, you're afraid of it happening again and you do all you can to prevent yourself from feeling that kind of pain again. That means not even contemplating marriage. I've come around, though. You did that for me."

He had a feeling she'd be the one to drive away his inability to trust. That feeling compelled him to begin to make his house suitable for a family, and also the next action he planned to take.

"You did something for me, too, Jaslene. You made me believe that love is still possible, that I should give it a second chance."

Reaching into his pocket, he knelt on one knee, looking up at her as he held a ring between his forefinger and his thumb. "Will you marry me?"

He expected her reaction to be one of shock. Her mouth opened with a sharp inhale and she stared at the round sapphire surrounded by several round diamonds. Since she was a geologist he didn't think she'd want anything too gaudy and flashy.

"Cal…"

Lifting her left hand, he slid the ring on her finger. "Will you marry me?"

She lifted her hand to stare some more at the ring. "This is so beautiful." She at last looked at him. "Are you sure about this?"

"No, and yes. I'm not sure I'm ready for marriage right now, but I am sure about you and the baby. I want to try and make this work."

"For the baby?"

"For all three of us and any other children that come along. I want a family. It's what I've always wanted. And… I love you."

She stared at him, hearing the truth in his tone. "Me, too. And I love you, too."

"Then you'll marry me?" The floor was beginning to get pretty hard.

After several seconds, she finally nodded a few times. Then she smiled. "Yes."

He stood up. She looped her arms over his shoulders and he pulled her close. Then he kissed her.

* * * * *

ROMANTIC suspense

Available October 1, 2019

#2059 COLTON FAMILY SHOWDOWN
The Coltons of Roaring Springs • by Regan Black
When Fox Colton finds a baby on his doorstep, he has no idea what to do. Luckily, his new assistant, Kelsey Lauder, was a nanny in college and is willing to share her skills. But when danger descends, will these two be able to set aside their baggage to protect the baby—and maybe find love along the way?

#2060 COLTON 911: DEADLY TEXAS REUNION
Colton 911 • by Beth Cornelison
While placed on leave, FBI agent Nolan Colton returns home to Whisperwood, Texas, and finds himself drawn into childhood friend—now a private investigator—Summer Davies's latest murder investigation. As they move in on their suspect, they grow close and risk their lives for love.

#2061 UNDER THE AGENT'S PROTECTION
Wyoming Nights • by Jennifer D. Bokal
Wyatt Thornton spent years searching for a killer—before dropping into hiding himself. Everly Baker's brother is the latest victim and she'll stop at nothing to get help from reclusive Wyatt. Together, can they trace the murderer—before evil gets to them first?

#2062 REUNITED BY THE BADGE
To Serve and Seduce • by Deborah Fletcher Mello
Attorney Simone Black has loved only one man, Dr. Paul Reilly. Parting ways broke both their hearts. Now Paul desperately needs Simone's help when he discovers something fatally wrong in the medications provided by a major pharmaceutical company. Can these two find their way back to each other while bringing down a powerful enemy?

Get 4 FREE REWARDS!

We'll send you 2 FREE Books plus <u>plus</u> 2 FREE Mystery Gifts.

Harlequin® Romantic Suspense books feature heart-racing sensuality and the promise of a sweeping romance set against the backdrop of suspense.

FREE Value Over $20

YES! Please send me 2 FREE Harlequin® Romantic Suspense novels and my 2 FREE gifts (gifts are worth about $10 retail). After receiving them, if I don't wish to receive any more books, I can return the shipping statement marked "cancel." If I don't cancel, I will receive 4 brand-new novels every month and be billed just $4.99 per book in the U.S. or $5.74 per book in Canada. That's a savings of at least 12% off the cover price! It's quite a bargain! Shipping and handling is just 50¢ per book in the U.S. and $1.25 per book in Canada.* I understand that accepting the 2 free books and gifts places me under no obligation to buy anything. I can always return a shipment and cancel at any time. The free books and gifts are mine to keep no matter what I decide.

240/340 HDN GNMZ

Name (please print)

Address   Apt. #

City   State/Province   Zip/Postal Code

Mail to the **Reader Service:**
IN U.S.A.: P.O. Box 1341, Buffalo, NY 14240-8531
IN CANADA: P.O. Box 603, Fort Erie, Ontario L2A 5X3

Want to try 2 free books from another series! Call 1-800-873-8635 or visit www.ReaderService.com.

"I appreciate you coming," he said.

"You said it was important."

Paul nodded as he gestured for her to take a seat. Sitting down, Simone stole another quick glance toward the bar. The two strangers were both staring blatantly, not bothering to hide their interest in the two of them.

Simone rested an elbow on the tabletop, turning flirtatiously toward her friend. "Do you know Tom and Jerry over there at the bar?" she asked softly. She reached a hand out, trailing her fingers against his arm.

Her touch was just distracting enough that Paul didn't turn abruptly to stare back, drawing even more attention in their direction. His focus shifted slowly from her toward the duo at the bar. He eyed them briefly before turning his attention back to Simone. He shook his head. "Should I?"

"It might be nothing, but they seem very interested in you."

Paul's gaze danced back in their direction and he took a swift inhale of air. One of the men was on a cell phone and both were still eyeing him intently.

"We need to leave," he said, suddenly anxious. He began to gather his papers.

"What's going on, Paul?"

"I don't think we're safe, Simone."

"What do you mean we're not safe?" she snapped, her teeth clenched tightly. "Why are we not safe?"

"I'll explain, but I think we really need to leave."

Simone took a deep breath and held it, watching as he repacked his belongings into his briefcase.

"We're not going anywhere until you explain," she started, and then a commotion at the door pulled at her attention.

Don't miss
Reunited by the Badge *by Deborah Fletcher Mello*
available October 2019 wherever
Harlequin® Romantic Suspense
books and ebooks are sold.

www.Harlequin.com

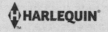

Love Harlequin romance?

DISCOVER.

Be the first to find out about promotions, news and exclusive content!

f Facebook.com/HarlequinBooks

t Twitter.com/HarlequinBooks

◉ Instagram.com/HarlequinBooks

p Pinterest.com/HarlequinBooks

ReaderService.com

EXPLORE.

Sign up for the Harlequin e-newsletter and download a free book from any series at **TryHarlequin.com.**

CONNECT.

Join our Harlequin community to share your thoughts and connect with other romance readers!
Facebook.com/groups/HarlequinConnection

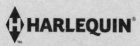

◈ HARLEQUIN®
™

**ROMANCE WHEN
YOU NEED IT**

Reward the book lover in you!

Earn points on your purchase of new Harlequin books from participating retailers.

Turn your points into **FREE BOOKS** of your choice!

Join for FREE today at
www.HarlequinMyRewards.com.

Harlequin My Rewards is a free program (no fees) without any commitments or obligations.